Dear Reader,

Midnight at Moonstone is a spell binding adventure
story set in a magical costume museum. Magical,
because on the stroke of midnight the mannequins
come to life…

Our hero, Kit, is staying at the museum, run by her
grumpy and distant grandfather. She is the only one
privy to the secrets of the Moonstone Museum and she
is the only one who can save the museum from closure
and the costumes from destruction!

A story set in a costume museum deserves a
sumptuous package so the book will be beautifully
illustrated by **Trisha Krauss** and we are producing a
gorgeous paperback cover with flaps. Author,
Lara Flecker, brings her own flair and authenticity
to proceedings: when she's not writing enchanting
children's fiction, she works as a Senior Conservation
Display Specialist at the V&A.

Midnight at Moonstone is at its heart a celebration
of creativity and Kit's great imagination, courage and
determination really shines through.

I hope you fall in love with this magical story, as I
have done. Happy reading!

Best wishes
Clare Whitston
Senior Commissioning Editor

OXFORD
UNIVERSITY PRESS

Great Clarendon Street, Oxford OX2 6DP

Oxford University Press is a department of the University of Oxford.
It furthers the University's objective of excellence in research, scholarship,
and education by publishing worldwide. Oxford is a registered trade mark
of Oxford University Press in the UK and in certain other countries

British Library Cataloguing in Publication Data

Data available

ISBN: 978-0-19-276889-6

1 3 5 7 9 10 8 6 4 2

Printed in Great Britain

Paper used in the production of this book is a natural,
recyclable product made from wood grown in sustainable forests.
The manufacturing process conforms to the environmental
regulations of the country of origin.

MIDNIGHT AT MOONSTONE

WRITTEN BY
LARA FLECKER

ILLUSTRATED BY
TRISHA KRAUSS

OXFORD
UNIVERSITY PRESS

The William Siddis Memorial School
London

August 1st

My Dear Sir Henry

It is with great regret that I am writing to you today
with some disappointing news. After due consideration,
we find that we are unable to award your daughter,
Katherine, a place at The William Siddis Memorial
School.

Following her poor performance in her initial
examination, it went against my better judgement to
allow Katherine to re-sit the tests. However, as you are
a member of the board of governors, I agreed to your
request. Indeed, given the extraordinary intellectual
abilities of your other children, I wondered if there
might have been some mistake. Sadly, having assessed

your daughter for a second time, I no longer have any doubts. Katherine is by no means unintelligent but she falls a long way short of the high academic standard required to attend William Siddis. As you know, we take only the very best.

I am sure you will agree that it will be better for all concerned if you select a more (for want of a better word) ordinary school for your daughter. I believe there are one or two highly satisfactory secondary institutions in your area that might suit her and I have no doubt she will do extremely well within the spectrum of her own, more average, capabilities.

I hope that your disappointment in this letter will be of short duration and I wish Katherine all the very best with her future.

Yours Sincerely

Malcomb Clapper (Head Teacher)

CHAPTER ONE

Kit Halliwell was hard at work in her bedroom. She was attempting to make an elaborately beaded mask for her older sister, Rosalind, who had been invited to a fancy-dress ball. Using a pair of fine-nosed tweezers from her mum's sewing box, she carefully picked up a tiny glittering bead and set it into the glue around the eye hole.

Kit raked nosily through the jar of beads, selected another and pressed it into place. Of course, the tweezers probably weren't designed for this kind of job. The ends were already clogged with glue and she would have to clean them carefully afterwards. Taking care of her mum's old sewing tools was a way of life for Kit, although she did wonder what the tweezers were doing there in the first place. They didn't seem to have a lot to do with needlework. It was one of the many questions that she wished she could ask her mum.

She held the mask at arm's length to see how it looked and, in the process, knocked a pile of newspaper onto the floor. Kit huffed in frustration. Her bedroom desk was hopeless for this kind of project. She needed a big work table, but what were the chances of that? Her dad would never agree. Anyway, there wasn't space in her room, not unless she got rid of something first.

Her eyes considered the furniture and came to rest on her doll's house. She hesitated. Maybe the time had come to say goodbye to this old friend? She was too old to play with it any more, and recently she'd been having a horrible recurring nightmare about being trapped inside it while the house was on fire. It was always the same. She was locked in the miniature room with the flowery wallpaper and would wake gasping for breath, with the smell of smoke still in her nostrils. Maybe if she got rid of the house, the dream would stop?

But what was she thinking of? Of course

she couldn't get rid of it. The doll's house had belonged to her mum and, for that reason alone, it was precious.

'I see you are hard at work,' said a voice, out of the blue.

Kit's head whipped round and there was her dad, Sir Henry Halliwell, standing in the doorway. He wasn't smiling.

'I'm making Roz a mask,' said Kit brightly, trying to hide her uneasiness. She held it up. 'What do you think?'

But Sir Henry's eyes remained fixed on her.

'Can Rosalind not buy a mask from a shop?'

'I wanted to give her a surprise, you know, make something special.'

'Special?' And now he did glance at the mask, but he looked away again almost immediately. Kit felt crushed. Would her dad ever be impressed by anything that she made?

'Stand up please, Katherine.'

Kit put the mask down and stood up warily. 'Would you mind casting your eye around this room? In particular, I would like to draw your attention to the desk.'

Kit glanced sideways and realized that she couldn't actually see any part of it under the chaos of newspaper, glue, scissors, and paint.

'Remind me what I purchased your desk for.'

'Studying,' mumbled Kit.

'And are you doing that now?'

'No.'

There was a powerful silence.

'You are twelve years old,' said Sir Henry quietly. 'Not a child at nursery, doing gluing and sticking.'

'Dad,' said Kit indignantly. 'This is not gluing and sticking. I'm making something,' but she had tried to explain this to him before and he had never listened yet.

'If you would stop wasting your time on all this craft nonsense, there would be more hours in the day for your school work.'

'Because I don't do nearly enough of that already,' she muttered to the floor.

'I beg your pardon?'

Kit wished she'd kept her mouth shut. Now she would have to explain herself and explaining things to her dad never went well.

'What I mean is that I already spend a lot of time studying. I do loads more than most of the kids in my class.'

'You are not most of the kids in your class,' said Sir Henry icily. 'Do you know what your brother and sister had accomplished by your age? Albert was already setting up his first business and Rosalind had been selected to speak at the international political youth summit.'

'I know,' agreed Kit. 'They were both amazing and incredible and . . . not really that normal, to be honest.'

'And, by contrast, what have you succeeded in doing? Failed your school entrance exam. Do you have any idea what an embarrassment that was for me?'

Kit winced. Was that really what she was to her world famous father? An embarrassment?

'Given that I am expecting to hear from William Siddis this very week, I would have thought you might try to behave as I wish for once.'

At mention of the school her hand flew to her back pocket, making sure that the letter was still there. She could feel the folded envelope sticking out of the top and tugged her shirt down to hide it.

'I'm not sure you realize how lucky you are, Katherine. As a rule, if you fail the entrance exam for a school like William Siddis, there are no second chances. As I am a governor, I've been able to pull a few strings for you.' He glanced at his watch. 'I must say I had hoped to hear from Malcomb Clapper before I leave for South America today, but there's been nothing.'

'M . . . M . . .' Kit swallowed and tried again.

'Maybe I'd be better off at St. Leopold's.'

'Excuse me?'

'It's got a good art department,' whispered Kit.

'ART DEPARTMENT!'

'Only if I don't get into Sidds, I mean,' said Kit. 'It could be, you know, a sort of plan B.'

Sir Henry stared with disbelief at his daughter. He was one of the world's most celebrated scientists, a genius. How could any child of his need a plan B?

'Look,' he said at last. 'I understand that you are more creative than your brother and sister, but unfortunately that kind of aptitude won't get you a job. I want you to have the same opportunities as Albert and Rosalind. Is that so unreasonable?'

'But what if Sidds doesn't want me?' said Kit desperately.

Sir Henry inhaled deeply and Kit could see the frustration in his face. 'If you have failed to get in for a second time, then I will collect together all this "making" paraphernalia of yours and put it in the dustbin, including that absurd sewing box you've become so attached to.'

'You can't do that,' said Kit angrily. 'It belonged to Mum.'

'No, well, perhaps not,' he conceded. 'But if you think that your mother wouldn't have been every bit as disappointed in you as I am, then you are wrong.'

He pulled a typed document from under his arm. 'Your itinerary for the next few weeks,' he said coldly and threw it across the room. It landed with neat accuracy on her desk, knocking the glue pot flying. 'I'll say goodbye then. The lodger will be in her room all day, so you won't be alone. Albert will pick you up at five this afternoon. Make sure you're ready.'

'OK,' said Kit. Then, unable to let him leave on a three-and-a-half-week filming trip with such bad feeling in the air, she added, 'Sorry, Dad.'

Sir Henry relented and held out an arm. She went to him immediately and gave him a hug.

'You know I only want the best for you,' he said, kissing the top of her head and hugging her back. 'Promise that you will at least try to put more effort into your studies while I'm away?'

'I will.'

'And then maybe we can look into . . . Oh for heaven's sake,' he snapped suddenly, noticing the paper strewn across the floor and the dripping glue. 'Look at the mess you've made. Please, make sure you tidy this room before you go.'

The door closed and Kit was left on her own feeling bitter. Whose fault was it that the glue had been knocked over? She turned back to the table and discovered that the glue pot had tipped over on to her mask. There was glue dripping through the eye holes and it was completely ruined.

She threw the mask into the bin, listening to the sound of Sir Henry's footsteps going downstairs. After that she could hear his wheeled suitcase being dragged down the hall. Then the front door slammed.

There was silence.

Kit moved over to the window and looked down. She was just in time to see the case being loaded into the boot of a taxi far below. She could see her dad through the car window, extracting papers from his brief case. He was already hard at work. Then the driver got in and the taxi drove off down the road.

With the car safely out of sight, Kit pulled the envelope from her back pocket. It was addressed to Sir Henry Halliwell and in the top left corner was the red crest of the William Siddis Memorial School. Kit looked away. She had no wish to read the letter again. Once had been enough. Certain phrases had been repeating themselves unpleasantly inside her head all morning – 'Poor performance', 'Falling a long way short', 'Average capabilities'.

She imagined her dad reading those words and shivered. Thank goodness she had found the letter before he had. She was safe, but not for long. In three and a half weeks' time, Sir Henry would return from filming his latest science programme and would have to know the truth, and what would he do then?

Kit returned to her desk and glanced down at the itinerary. From the look of page one, it was just as bad as all the others.

AUGUST ITINERARY		
DATE	LOCATION	ADDITIONAL NOTES
3rd – 7th August	Albert	Be packed and ready in advance. Albert will pick you up promptly at 5.
7th – 11th August	Rosalind	Rosalind will give you extra maths coaching in the evenings. Please take your books.
11th – 13th August	Agency	A nanny from the Agency will babysit.
13th – 16th August	Albert	Albert will be entertaining some important clients on Friday. Make sure you are quiet and keep out of the way.

AUGUST ITINERARY		
DATE	**LOCATION**	**ADDITIONAL NOTES**
18th – 22nd August	Agency	A different nanny from the Agency will babysit.
22nd – 27th August	Rosalind	Not ideal timing for Rosalind who is under a lot of stress at work. She has three evening engagements, but will set some maths and English for you to occupy yourself with while she is out.

Kit's mum had died when she was a baby and, as long as she could remember, her life had been ruled by itineraries. Sir Henry must have written hundreds of them over the years, all printed out neatly on spreadsheets, with dates, and times, and countless additional notes. Kit imagined how different things would have been if her mum was still alive, and a familiar aching longing came over her.

Kit picked up the document and half-heartedly tried to wipe off the glue that had spilt down one side. As she did so, however, she noticed that her mum's open sewing box had also been splattered with the stuff. It was all over the pin cushion and the thimble was brimming with white paste, like a miniature cup of milk.

Kit had been upset before, but now she was burning with rage. It was bad enough that Rosalind's mask had been ruined, but damage to her mum's beloved sewing box was ten times worse. She snatched up the stapled sheets of the itinerary and ripped them down the middle. Then she tore them in half again and again, shredding them into tiny bits so there was no chance of ever being able to put it back together.

This felt so good that she did the same to the school rejection letter, letting the fragments flutter around her like confetti – 'Read that if you can, Dad!'

By the time she'd finished, the fury inside her had cooled, but it didn't disappear. It hardened into something else and she was filled with a determination that was new to her. She was surprised to find that, without even thinking about it, she had made a decision. She had never fitted in to her family, not properly, and she knew exactly what she was going to do. It was time to run away.

She reached under her bed, pulled out an old backpack and started stuffing things into it. Jeans, socks, pants, sweaters. She grabbed her toothbrush from the bathroom and her pyjamas from her bed. Finally she turned to the sewing box on her desk and, for the first

time, she hesitated. What would her mum
think about her running away? Surely she
would have understood? Inside something was
niggling at her uncomfortably. She knew what
she was doing was wrong, but she pushed the
thought away and concentrated on cleaning up
the sewing box instead. Then she put all her
emergency money in to it for safe keeping.

Before she closed the box and packed it, she
slid her hand inside a pocket in the lining and
pulled out an old leaflet. She would be needing

this because it had the address of where she was
going. For a moment she gazed at the tattered
pamphlet. On the front was a faded picture
of an old historic house, the home where her
mum had grown up. How many years had she
been dreaming about visiting? She had always

believed that here was a place that she might actually fit in, somewhere she could belong, just like her mum. She traced a finger over the name, aware of the mysterious tingle it always gave her. Moonstone Costume Museum.

Ignoring the mess on her desk, Kit folded the leaflet carefully and put it in her pocket. Now she was almost ready to go. There was just one important thing still to do. She had to tell some lies.

* * *

Downstairs in the kitchen, Kit picked up her phone nervously and then put it down again. She wasn't experienced with dishonesty and this was going to take a bit of planning. There were three people she had to lie to. One was the receptionist at the nanny agency and the other two were her brother and sister.

She decided to begin with the agency. Wiping sweaty palms down her front, she listened to make sure the lodger was still safely in her room, then lifted the phone once more.

'Hi. I'm Sir Henry Halliwell's personal assistant and I'm calling to let you know that he won't be requiring the services of your agency for the foreseeable future. Please cancel all nanny engagements until further notice. Goodbye.'

Phew! That hadn't been so bad. Maybe this wasn't going to be as difficult as she had expected. Feeling encouraged, Kit rang her brother. As usual, he didn't pick up. He was much too busy being an entrepreneur to answer a call from his little sister, so she left a message.

'Ummmm . . . Hi Albert . . . er . . . I'm calling to let you know that Dad's changed the August itinerary because . . . well, I'm not really sure why, but anyway he has and, er . . . I'm not coming to stay any more, I'll go to Roz instead . . . so that's good news, isn't it . . . for you I mean, not for me . . . not that it's bad news for me, I love staying with Roz . . . it's really great . . . er . . . Right, well, see you in September I guess . . . Oh by the way, it's your sister, I mean it's Kit.'

By the end of this message Kit felt hot all over and her confidence had completely evaporated. Lying to her brother turned out to be horrible, and there was still Rosalind to come. Kit wasn't taking any chances this time, so she wrote herself a script and practised for ten minutes before taking the plunge. As expected, Rosalind didn't answer her phone either. She was much too busy working for the government as a political adviser, so Kit left a message.

'Hi Roz, it's me, Kit. Sorry to bother you when you're busy, but Dad asked me to pass on a message about this month's itinerary. He's really worried that you are working too hard and has decided that it's not fair to expect you to look after me as well, so I'll be staying with Albert instead and you are Kit-free for the rest of August.

'Oh yes, and don't worry about the maths coaching, Albert has promised to give me loads and he's going to give me extra English and extra science every day. It's going to be . . . woops!' (Kit had accidently knocked the script off the table.) 'Great . . . er . . . anyway . . . I hope your cold is better now,' (crawling on hands and knees to try and retrieve it.) 'Umm, and your sore throat isn't . . . er . . . sore any more. OK, well, bye for now and don't worry about where I am . . . I mean, obviously I'll be with Albert, so that's fine . . . Bye.'

Kit collapsed where she was under the table and groaned. How come the rest of the world seemed able to lie without any trouble? She wriggled out from between the chair legs and brushed the toast crumbs off her knees. Now there was just her dad to deal with, but this was going to be easy by comparison. She planned to leave him a note and, as he was safely in South America for the next three and a half weeks, he wouldn't even read it until he was back.

She found a pad and pencil and, after a moment, started scribbling. The note didn't take long and when it was finished she put it in an envelope and left it on the table. She took a last look around the kitchen, wondering when she would see it again. If everything went according to plan, it wouldn't be any time soon. Then she picked up her bag and, without even bothering to let the lodger know, she walked straight out of the front door.

Dad,

I've had enough, so have gone to stay with my grandfather at Moonstone.

Kit x

CHAPTER TWO

It wasn't until evening that Kit finally reached
Moonstone, after a long and exhausting journey.
A summer gale had whipped up out of nowhere
and she glimpsed the old house for the first time
through driving rain.

It looked a grim and sinister place in the
storm, waiting for her at the end of a long,
potholed drive. Kit had never actually been
here before and her mum's old leaflet revealed
nothing of this bleak loneliness. The windows
were like empty voids in the stone façade, black
and lifeless. She shivered and suddenly wished
that she could go home, but it was getting dark
and she was in the middle of nowhere. She had
no choice but to go on.

She rolled her aching shoulders inside the straps of her backpack, then trudged on again, while the wind filled her ears with its raging and flung handfuls of rain at her cheeks. There wasn't far to go now, but she had to pick her way carefully to avoid all the puddles. Everything around her seemed depressingly run down. The gravel under foot was clotted with weeds, the flower beds overgrown and tangled with ivy, and as she got closer to the house, she could see that this too was in bad shape. There were broken slates on the roof, the paintwork was peeling and several windows had been boarded up.

Kit crept up to the front door. On it was a torn card held in place by a rusty nail. Straining her eyes, she could just make out the faded words—

MOONSTONE COSTUME MUSEUM

OPENING HOURS:

TUESDAY TO SUNDAY—TEN O'CLOCK TO FIVE O'CLOCK.

CLOSED ON MONDAYS.

She checked her watch—nine fifteen. The museum had already been shut for more than four hours. If only she could have got here sooner. She looked nervously at the vast door, weathered grey with age. This would have been

so much easier if it was already open and there were members of the general public coming and going. Her grandfather ran the museum and he might have been standing right here at the entrance, ready to welcome her. Now she was going to have to ring the bell, only there was no bell, just a tarnished old knocker that looked as if it was about to fall off.

Kit lifted it carefully and smacked it as hard as she dared, once, twice, three times, then she stepped back and waited.

She remained there for a long time. At last, a dim light appeared in some of the lower windows and, not long afterwards, a loud grating noise began, as if someone on the other side of the door was wrestling with a pair of rusty bolts. The sound added an ominous soundtrack to an already nerve-racking wait, but eventually the door was pushed open a crack and the surly face of an old man peered out from the darkness.

'What do you want this time of night?' he said gruffly. 'You one of Finn Scudder's lot?'

'Er . . .' said Kit. 'I'm . . . My name is Kit.'

The old man suddenly pushed the door wider.

'Well, who in the name of heaven is this? By Jove! Will you look at that! A girl! A titchy little girl knocking on my door.'

'Good afternoon.'

'Afternoon!' repeated the old man 'You call this afternoon, do you? It's ten o'clock at blasted night.'

'Only nine fifteen,' said Kit.

'And that makes all the difference, does it?'

Kit shook her head uncertainly. She didn't think she was getting off to a very good start with her grandfather, if that was who he was, but how was she supposed to know? She hadn't seen him since she was a baby. She'd always imagined that he looked a bit like Father Christmas, but there wasn't much of a Santa Clause twinkle about this irritable old man.

'Are you Bernard Trench?'

'None of your business. What I want to know is how the blazes you got here?'

'I came on a bus. You know, from London.'

'No bus from anywhere comes down this way, let alone London.'

'I got a bus to the nearest town,' explained Kit. 'Then I walked.'

The old man stared. 'You're never telling me that you've walked all the way from Axly?'

'I didn't have enough money for a taxi, so I bought a map instead. It took much longer than I thought. It only looked about three centimetres.'

'It's all of ten miles, you daft little fool,' said the man. 'What did you want to traipse all the way out here for?'

'To see you, of course,' said Kit, and then added: 'That is, if you are Bernard Trench. Maybe it would help if I told you who I am.'

'Don't bother.'

'But—'

'Look, I don't know what you think you're up to, but I want you off my premises sharpish or I'll call the police' and the old man started to pull the heavy door shut again.

'The thing is, I think I'm kind of a relation to you,' squeaked Kit as the old man disappeared from view.

'Don't talk nonsense, I don't have relations,' and the door closed with a hefty clunk. A second later came the rasping sound of the bolts again.

Kit was now in a flat panic. He'd shut the door on her, he had actually shut the door! So much for coming to a place where she might belong. What kind of a man was her grandfather? Where was the warm welcome and the Christmassy beard? Not even Sir Henry would slam the door in a child's face on a night like this. Kit looked helplessly at her surroundings. The wind was keening around the corners of the house, the trees clattering their branches in the near darkness. She'd probably die of exposure if she stayed out here all night.

In desperation she felt for the keyhole with her finger and pressed her lips to it. There didn't seem much chance she would be heard over the wind and the rain and the interminable grinding bolts, but she had to give it a go. She took a big breath and bawled at the top of her voice, 'I'M YOUR GRANDDAUGHTER.'

Instantly the bolts were drawn back and the door opened again. The eyes of the old man were staring out at her once more, but this time there was something like recognition in his expression.

'You're . . . you're Emmi's youngest,' his voice trembled.

'Yes,' Kit was breathless with relief.

'That titchy little baby?'

'You remember me?'

'I can see you look a bit like her now.'

'Do I?' People had said this to her often before, but she never got tired of hearing it. 'I don't think we've met since Mum's funeral. Not that I can remember it because I was only one, but Dad told me about it once.'

At the mention of Sir Henry, her grandfather's expression hardened.

'Well, this is all I need,' growled the old man,

reverting back to his previous manner.

'Er . . . pleased to meet you,' said Kit, attempting to smile.

'Well I'm not,' he said. 'What are you doing here?"

"I've come on a v . . . visit.'

He eyed her bag suspiciously. 'Have you come all the way here on your own? How old are you?'

"Oh, you know, about fifteen!' said Kit vaguely.

'D'you think I was born yesterday?'

"Well OK, more like going on fourteen."

"You mean you're thirteen."

'Nearly thirteen!'

The old man rolled his eyes upward. 'Ruddy marvellous. And I suppose that rotten old father of yours doesn't know you're here?'

'He's in South America.'

'Course he is.' The old man exhaled irritably and looked her over. 'S'pose you'll have to stop here for the night then.'

'Oh, thank you. That's really kind. Thank you so mu—'

'It'll only be for the one night, mind.'

Kit followed him inside and then, trying to be helpful, attempted to close the door.

'Stand back, will you,' he snapped. 'I need to see to the locks. There's valuable stuff in this museum.'

The door closed once more, but this time, thank goodness, she was on the inside. Then an ear-splitting screeching sound began as her grandfather went into battle with the bolts all over again. It was ten times worse when you were standing next to them. Kit winced.

'Maybe, you know, some oil might help with that,' she suggested.

'And you've got some handy, have you?' shouted the old man sarcastically over the racket.

Kit thought sadly of the bottle of WD-40 she always kept for emergencies at home. Then she had a brainwave. She felt in her pocket and pulled out a stick of lip balm. Uncapping it, she slipped under her grandfather's arm and began running it up and down the rusty bolt he was currently grappling with.

'What the heck . . . !'

'Try now,' said Kit.

The old man gave her a filthy look and nudged half-heartedly at the shaft of corroded metal. The bolt immediately shot into place and Kit beamed.

'Have you quite finished meddling?' said the old man.

'S . . . sorry.' She returned the lip balm to her pocket.

'Right then, you'd better follow me and make sure you keep your hands to yourself. There are important artefacts in here and you're not to touch anything.'

* * *

it was dark inside, but Kit could tell that she was in some kind of vast entrance hall. Their footsteps came back to her in little echoing whispers as if there were more than just the two of them walking across the floor. Countless shadowy portraits chequered the walls and here and there she caught sight of a spectral face staring out from a gilded frame. They gave Kit the shivers.

As her eyes got used to the gloom, she became aware of something else. The place seemed familiar, as if she had been there before. It took her a few moments to understand why this should be, but suddenly her doll's house flashed into her mind and she realized how similar the hall in it was to the one she was now walking through. Both had the same wood panelling and floor boards, along with an unusual double staircase that twisted up to a railed balcony above. For a moment she felt dizzy and disorientated, as if her nightmare was coming true. She sniffed to make sure there was no smell of smoke.

It soon became obvious to Kit that this couldn't be a coincidence. Her mum's old doll's house must be some kind of a miniature replica of the costume museum, although it didn't appear to be an exact copy. The proportions of the hall were different. The real Moonstone was also in a much worse condition than her doll's house at home. She could see signs of damage everywhere; the large mirror above the fireplace, with a jagged crack running across it, broken banister rods on the staircase, the central chandelier draped with cobwebs, and an unpleasant crunching underfoot, which suggested that the floor hadn't been washed in a while. Kit could only imagine how much worse the place would look in daylight. What exactly had been going on at Moonstone for it to get into this mess? Had it been like this when her mum lived here?

To the left of the staircase was a door, invitingly ajar. It would only take a second to look inside and she might not get another chance. She glanced at her grandfather, who was now stomping laboriously up the stairs in front of her. He hadn't looked back once since they'd set off—he'd never notice if she disappeared for a moment.

Kit veered off sideways and slipped quickly through the opening. Then she froze.

There were people inside, three shadowy figures, standing right in front of her. The shock was horrifying, but then she realized her mistake. She was in a costume museum, remember, and these strangely motionless forms standing on little pedestals were not real people, they were just historic clothes worn by dummies. Weak with relief, she took a few steps forward and then hesitated.

The moon had broken through the clouds for a moment and shone through the window, illuminating the costumes with a ghostly radiance. It was silly to be scared of a few mannequins dressed in old clothes, but in that eerie light, they looked so realistic. Their eyes seemed to follow her.

She glanced uneasily over her shoulder and then inched further in.

The room had an oriental flavour to it and the costumes were unexpectedly exotic. At first she thought they were all female, but then she realized that two of the mannequins were men. No wonder she was confused, they looked like they were wearing dresses. One was in a gold wrap-over tunic with a wide skirt, while the other seemed to be wearing some kind of long white nightie. It had weird elongated sleeves that dangled down on either side and was tied at the waist with a bulky scarf.

The only female figure also appeared to be in nightwear, although in her case this was a glamorous looking dressing gown, which dropped from her narrow shoulders in a sweep of lavishly patterned fabric.

Just then Kit heard a slight rustle and thought she saw something move over on the right. She swung round to find that there was a fourth costume in the room. It was tucked away in the shadows, half out of sight, behind a screen—an odd place to display a garment.

This costume was neither a man nor a woman, but a young girl. She looked only a little older than Kit. Her gown was made of a soft mushroom-coloured silk woven with flowers. There were lace ruffles at her elbows, a delicate a shawl around her shoulders and the skirt was open at the front, revealing a pink petticoat. Kit had a feeling that she was looking at something that was hundreds of years old.

The figure looked unhappy. The lace drooped and the motionless face stared blindly across the room. Kit put out a hand towards her . . .

'OI!' It was the old man. He must have finally twigged that she wasn't following and come back to look for her. 'WHAT DO YOU THINK YOU'RE DOING?'

'Nothing,' said Kit.

'Didn't I tell you to follow me and not to touch? Ooo, you've got a nerve. You turn up here in the middle of the night and as soon as you're through the door, you're up to no good. Do you understand English?'

'Yes, yes I do.'

'Then follow me AND DON'T TOUCH.'

Kit scurried after him, making sure that she kept close this time. He led her up to the first floor, followed by more stairs and then along a dark passage. At last they arrived at a door and passed into what appeared to be her grandfather's private living quarters.

'You'll have to sleep in your mum's old room, I suppose,' he muttered. They set off up yet another flight of steps. 'No one's stopped in here since she left to get married to that man.' And he opened a low white door and led her into an attic bedroom.

Kit loved it on sight. The room was cleaner and in better repair than anything else she'd seen at Moonstone. It had cream walls, a dormer window with long curtains and an actual fireplace. The old wooden bed was covered with a worn patchwork quilt and there was a large table pushed into one corner. Just being there made Kit feel closer to her mother.

'Was this really my mum's room?'

'I said so, didn't I?'

Kit turned slowly around, hoping to find some of her mother's old belongings, but the room was stripped and empty except for a strange looking picture on the wall above the bed. She moved closer and saw that it was a hand-drawn map of the costume museum.

'Who drew this? It's beautiful,' asked Kit.

Her grandfather didn't reply, just nodded in the direction of a chest of drawers.

'There's sheets and such like in there, you'll have to make up your own bed. The bathroom's downstairs. And make sure you're up early in the morning. I'll be taking you to the coach station first thing.'

'All right,' said Kit. 'Thanks for letting me stay.'

The old man grunted and turned to go. At the door he paused and, without looking round, said, 'It was your Mum drew that map. I framed it for her on her twelfth birthday.' Then he shuffled out of the room and closed the door firmly behind him.

Left alone, Kit found the sheets, made up the bed and switched off the light. Despite being exhausted she couldn't sleep, and for a long time she lay awake, listening to the sound of the wind gusting through the trees outside.

* * *

Kit must have dropped off because she was awoken suddenly by a noise, and knew right away there was someone in her room. Somewhere a clock was chiming persistently.

'Rosalind?' she said, so fuddled with sleep that she'd forgotten where she was.

There was something unfamiliar about the night. It was never this dark in London. No matter whose house or flat she was staying in, there were always street lights glowing through the curtains. Then she felt a draft of air and with it came the whiff of raw green leaves.

'Grandfather?' she breathed.

There was a soft rustle of clothing and then the creak of a floor board.

'Who's there?' said Kit, her voice barbed with fear. Her eyes struggled with the darkness, straining to see, but at the same time not really wanting to.

There came again that swish of fabric. The hinge of her door peeped slightly and was followed by the faint easing of carefully laid steps, descending the attic stairs. The sound receded and was lost but Kit was left gripping the side of her bed, too terrified even to put the light on.

There had been someone in her room, she was absolutely certain of it, and it wasn't the old man because she could hear him snoring in his bedroom.

So who was it? Kit fretted, lying rigid in the darkness. The only conclusion she could come to was that Moonstone, on top of everything else, was haunted.

CHAPTER 3

The storm was still going when Kit woke up the next morning. She could hear the rain striking the glass and could even feel wafts of air as the wind blasted against the rotten window frame.

She lay in bed recounting all the dreadful things that had happened the day before.

1. The horrible letter from the school.
2. Sir Henry's anger.
3. The depressing itinerary for her summer holidays.
4. Her disastrous arrival at Moonstone.
5. The ghostly sounds in her bedroom.

Kit looked bleakly out of the window. She had been fantasizing about her mum's old home for as long as she could remember. In her imagination it had always seemed such a magical place, a sanctuary. But now she was here, Kit realized how silly she'd been. Moonstone was nothing but a crumbling ruin, full of broken things, and her grandfather a heartless old man who couldn't wait to see the back of her. What would there be for her to dream about now?

Kit's only option was to go back to London, and that meant admitting to her brother and sister that she had lied to them. This prospect made her feel so wretched that she considered having another shot at persuading her grandfather. Maybe, if she explained everything to him clearly, he would change his mind?

BANG! BANG! BANG!

'Oi! Are you up yet?'

Kit flinched and clutched the bed covers around her neck. 'Umm . . . nearly—I'll be down in five minutes.'

'Well, get a blasted move on, will you? You've got to be in Axly soon to catch the bus.'

After that she could hear him stamping off down the stairs as if his feet were angry with the floorboards. So much for persuading him to change his mind.

She edged reluctantly out of bed and began picking up her clothes, which were still damp. She put them on anyway and tried to think of something positive about going back to London. At least her brother and sister didn't live in houses that were haunted. Kit paused for a moment, sock in hand and thought about the sounds she had heard in the night. Had she imagined them? Had there really been someone in her room? She would never know now.

She made the bed neatly, smoothing the patchwork quilt and had a last look round her mum's old room. She would probably never see it again and wanted to press the image of it into her memory—bed, fireplace, big table, window overlooking the gardens, her mum's map of the museum. Kit touched the frame and ran a finger over the dusty glass. 'Bye, Mum.'

* * *

'Call that five minutes, do you?' said the old man when she had located him in the kitchen at the bottom of the attic stairs. 'You've got a funny sense of time.' He was busy at the grill. 'We'll have to get off quick. The London coach leaves at eight thirty and I won't have any peace till I know you're on it. Here, take that,'—hurling a piece of toast across the table at her. 'Slap something on it and bring it with you, there's no time for breakfast.'

Kit fingered the toast hopelessly.

'Come on, get on with it.'

'Sorry, I'm just a bit tired,' mumbled Kit.

'Well whose fault's that? No one asked you to travel half way across the country and then walk ten miles in the middle of the night! Now put something on that toast or you'll have to eat it dry.'

'If it's OK, I don't really want it.'

'Suit yourself.'

He glanced sideways at her, but when he saw that she was looking, his eyes snapped away again and he pretended to look for his car keys. He picked them up and jangled them in her face. 'We can leave right now then, can't we? Sooner the better, far as I'm concerned.'

Kit picked up her bag and followed him out of the door. She was right about one thing, Moonstone did look worse in daylight. She was shocked by how bad it really was and wondered what the general public made of it?

As they made their way through the hall, they passed the room she'd explored last night. The door was wide open and she could see the mannequins standing in their places. The screen came into view and Kit looked eagerly for the girl in the mushroom-coloured gown, but there was no sign of her. She stopped for a second, puzzled.

'What are you up to?' said her Grandfather suspiciously.

'I was just wondering what happened to the . . . nothing,' said Kit.

* * *

The drive to Axly was carried out in complete silence. Did it ever stop raining here? Bare hills rose up steeply on either side of them and the narrow road twisted like unravelled knitting along the valley floor. As their journey progressed, their speed increased. It was as if the old man couldn't get her out of his car quick enough. Even when they arrived in Axly he hurtled through the little market town as if he was taking the Devil to the bus stop instead of his twelve-year-old granddaughter.

'Here we are,' he said, bringing the vehicle to a screeching stop. He sounded unflatteringly relieved. 'You've got a return ticket, have you?'

She shook her head and then blurted out; 'I don't think I've got enough money.'

'Course you haven't. Good job you came on this trip so well prepared,' he said sarcastically.

While her grandfather rooted around for some cash in the pocket of the car door, Kit opened her pack and lifted out the sewing box where her money was stored. She put it on her lap and counted out her remaining change. It didn't amount to much, certainly not a bus ticket all the way back to London.

She was suddenly aware that the old man had gone very silent. She looked up to find him staring at her as if he had seen a ghost.

'What . . . ?' said Kit uncertainly.

'Her old sewing box. I've not seen that for, I don't know how many years. Your mum left it to you, did she?'

'My brother and sister aren't really the sewing type,' said Kit, 'so they let me have it, not that I know how to sew either. Dad won't let me learn because he thinks it's a waste of time.'

'I made that box for Emmie when she was about your age.'

'You made it?' Kit was astonished.

The old man cleared his throat and looked down at the crumpled notes he now held in his hands as if he didn't know how they had got there. 'Well, here you are,' he said, handing them to her, 'That'll be enough to get you back to London. And you'd better have a few coins, just in case.'

'I'll pay you back. I'll borrow the money from Dad when he gets home and post it to you,' said Kit.

'Don't bother. I don't want nothing from him. You'd better get a move on, coach leaves in ten minutes. You can buy a ticket from the driver.'

Kit got slowly out of car and shivered in the damp wind.

'Thanks for the lift,' she said bleakly.

'Go on, hop it.' He nodded in the direction of the bus shelter and she trailed off across the wet tarmac, her backpack slung over one shoulder.

The orange plastic seat in the bus stop was about as welcoming as a barbed wire fence. The rain wept and trickled down the dirty glass and collected in little rock pools at her feet. Kit was not someone who cried much, but she felt so miserable at that moment that she was dangerously close to it. Luckily, someone else arrived before her tears got started and she pulled herself together. The last thing she wanted was some stranger taking pity on her and asking questions. She sniffed resolutely and kept her head down so she wouldn't have to look at the newcomer.

'So you want to learn how to sew, do you?' said a gruff voice.

Kit looked up and there was her grandfather standing right in front of her, with one foot in a puddle, his shoulders hunched like an old vulture and his hands dug deep in his pockets.

She nodded.

'And your dad doesn't see the worth of it?'

Kit nodded again. She was confused. What was he doing here? He should be on his way back to Moonstone. By this point, her expectations of him were pretty low. Maybe he didn't trust her to get on the bus and wanted to make absolutely sure. Then he did something even more surprising. He took one hand out of his pocket, picked up Kit's backpack and, without even looking at her, strode off back towards his Land Rover.

Kit stared, bewildered. Her grandfather appeared to be stealing her bag.

'Well, come on, then,' he called irritably. He seemed to know without even turning his head that she was still sitting like a potato on the bus stop seat. 'I can't wait around for you all day. I've got a museum to run.'

'You mean . . .' she hesitated in case she'd got it wrong. 'You mean I can come back with you?'

'Just for a day or two,' he said tersely. 'And as long as you promise to stay out of my way and keep those meddlesome little fingers of yours from messing with anything in the galleries.'

'I promise,' said Kit. 'I won't touch a thing, I

swear.'

'And you're to let that father of yours know where you are. I'm not having you staying at Moonstone without his permission. D'you understand?'

'Oh, yes, of course, definitely. I'll send him a message straight away.'

'Humph!' He threw her pack into the back of the Land Rover and slammed his way into the driving seat. Kit didn't wait for a second invitation, but got in beside him before he could change his mind.

* * *

The return journey looked as if it was going to be nearly as silent as the one before. Kit was nervous of doing anything that would annoy her grandfather and spent the first ten minutes trying to think of something safe to say.

'You don't half fidget,' complained the old man.

'Sorry,' said Kit. She felt in her pocket and pulled out her phone.

'What are you doing now?'

'Just sending my dad a message like you asked.'

There was silence again while she typed.

'There,' she said at last, switching her phone off and zipping it away in the pocket of her bag.

'You've sent it, have you?'

'Yep.' Which was true . . . to a certain extent. The fact was, although she had written and sent the message, it was very unlikely that her dad would ever see it. Sir Henry was always far too busy being a celebrity scientist to read any communications from his youngest daughter.

'And did you tell him that it was none of my doing?'

''Yes,' said Kit, ignoring the twinge of guilt. 'I said that it was all my idea and that you wouldn't let me stay at Moonstone unless I told him where I was, and I asked him to let Albert and Rosalind know as well. Does that sound OK?'

The old man grunted. Keen to change the subject, Kit racked her brain for something to say. 'Thank you so much for letting me stay Gr . . . Grandfather. It's really kind of you.'

The Land Rover swerved dangerously.

'What did you just call me?

'Grandfather,' repeated Kit nervously.

'Thought so. Well, don't never let me hear you say that again.' He shuddered. 'Ooo, makes me feel like some rusty old antique in one of those OAP homes.'

'Oh, OK. What shall I call you, then?'

'S'pose you'll have to call me Bernard.'

'Bernard,' Kit was taken aback. 'I can't call you that.'

'Why not? It's my name.'

'Could I maybe call you Grandpa instead?'

'That's supposed to be better, is it?'

'Granddad?'

The old man looked revolted.

'OK . . . Umm . . . what about Pop?'

'Pop! Think I'd rather shut myself up in a coffin right now.'

Kit had run out of ideas.

'Tell you what,' said the old man after an uncomfortable silence. 'You can call me Bard if you like. It's what the others . . . I mean, it's what my missus used to call me. She sort of made it up out of Bur and nard. Not sure how. Anyway, I don't mind being called Bard, if that suited you.'

'Bard,' Kit tested the name out. She liked it.

Just then, they turned into the drive of the museum. Bard slowed down and began zigzagging laboriously from side to side to avoid the potholes. The front of Moonstone came into view.

'Oh look, the museum's got a visitor,' said Kit pointing at a man in a black raincoat. 'Isn't it a bit early for opening?'

The man had his back to them and appeared to be studying the building, but he turned round as the vehicle approached and raised a lazy hand.

'I don't believe it,' snarled Bard putting his foot suddenly and violently on the accelerator. 'He's got a nerve coming here.' The Land Rover smashed through the potholes, spraying water in every direction.

'Who is it?' asked Kit, holding on to the door handle for dear life.

'Finn blasted Scudder.'

'What's—ow—what's wrong with him?'

'He's a scoundrel, that's what's wrong with him. He's a lying, cheating, property developer.'

'Property developer?' Kit was startled. 'What's a property developer doing here?'

'What d'you think he's doing here?' said Bard. 'He's trying to get his hands on this place of course. He wants to buy Moonstone.'

CHAPTER 4

The Land Rover came to a skidding halt a few feet from the man, splashing water over his trousers. He stood his ground, his thin ferrety face smiling arrogantly.

'What d'you want?' said Bard, wrenching his door open and climbing down.

'And good morning to you, Mr Trench' said Finn Scudder, sounding like a caricature of a dodgy businessman. 'That's an unusual way you have of greeting your visitors.'

'What?' Bard banged the door so violently behind him that Kit felt the Land Rover shake.

'Just a little tip from me. If you want to bring in the punters, try not to mow them down on the doorstep.'

'I asked what you're doing here.'

'Well, obviously, I've come to have a look round the museum, same as any other member of the public.'

'The museum's closed.'

Finn glanced at his wrist, pushing back the sleeve and revealing a flashy watch.

'I don't mind waiting, only I thought it might be less embarrassing for you, Mr Trench, if I inspected my future property when the place wasn't full of tourists.' Finn smiled nastily, 'Mind you, there's not likely to be anyone else here today, is there? What's the grand total of your visitor figures this month? Zero?'

The colour in Bard's leathery face darkened. He looked just about ready to explode, but Kit chose this moment to open the passenger door and climb out of the Land Rover. Up until this point she had remained unnoticed inside, wondering what to do. Her sudden appearance seemed to take both men by surprise, but Finn was soon finding the presence of a child at Moonstone a cause for added amusement.

'Hey up,' he said, pretending to look frightened. 'Looks like backup's arrived. I'd better watch my step.'

'Get back in the car,' muttered Bard, but Kit stayed put.

'Who's your little helper, mate?'

'I'm his granddaughter,' said Kit, trying to stop her voice wobbling.

'I said get back in the car.'

'Granddaughter? Really?' This time Finn looked genuinely taken aback. 'D'you know, I'd always put you down as a confirmed bachelor, Mr Trench. Don't tell me you actually had a wife and children once upon a time.'

Bard clenched his fists. Kit could practically feel the rage pumping out of him, like a rusty old radiator giving off heat.

'I want you off my premises now, Finn Scudder, or I'll call the police.'

'Ahh, but, unfortunately for you, mate, these aren't your premises, are they?' said Finn. 'Until I buy the place, Moonstone is owned by the council and you are nothing more than a substandard caretaker.'

He slid his hand inside his coat and took out a folded sheet of paper, which he shook open. 'If you read that, you'll see that I have authorization to view this property out of hours—so are you going to unlock the door, or do I need to call the police?'

He thrust the sheet of paper towards Bard, who took it reluctantly. Kit held her breath while the old man looked it over, but whatever it said must have convinced him, because after a moment he dug around in his pocket and pulled out the keys. Without a word, Bard unlocked the huge front door, pushed it open and stood back to let Finn pass.

'How long'll you be?'

Finn shrugged, swaggered arrogantly through the door and disappeared from view.

* * *

Kit looked at her grandfather in disbelief. 'You're not going to let that man just wander around on his own?'

'What do you want me to do? Help him measure up?'

'But he's . . . he's . . .' Kit struggled to find a bad enough word, '. . . awful! You can't let him buy Moonstone.'

'Don't have much choice, do I? Like he says, I don't own the place.'

Kit was silent. She was struggling to revise yet another of her preconceptions about the museum. The truth was that she had always assumed that her grandfather did own it.

'So Moonstone belongs to the council?' said Kit, wanting to make sure that she understood.

''S right.'

'But you've been running the place for years, haven't you? Doesn't that give you some rights over what happens?'

'Nope. If council want to sell, then that's up to them. Not much I can do about it.'

He seemed so matter-of-fact that Kit began to feel annoyed.

'But don't you mind?'

'Mind?' said Bard, 'Course I mind. Spent the best part of my life in this place. Fifty odd years I've been here, and you ask me if I mind.'

'Sorry.'

There was an awkward pause, during which, Bard rooted out a filthy looking handkerchief and honked loudly into it. He returned the rag to his pocket, then pivoted slowly on the spot until he was staring off into the distance.

'Come to Moonstone as a newlywed, I did.' he said, addressing some far-off hills. 'My missus persuaded me into it. She was related in some helter-skelter fashion to the Silk-Hattons that once owned this place, so she'd known it all her life. Anyway, turned out the local authority was looking for someone to take Moonstone on. 'Community Management' they call it nowadays.'

'What's that?' asked Kit, edging around slightly, so that she wasn't speaking directly to his back.

'It's a way of off-loading responsibility for an institution onto some poor chump in the local community. Saves the council from having to pay proper wages and avoids bad press for closing museums down. Everyone's at it these days, but we were well ahead of the game.'

'So you came to Moonstone to run the museum for free?'

'Well, job came with accommodation, of course, and we got paid a bit of a stipend, plus the museum gets an annual funding allowance, which hardly buys a tin of paint these days. After that, though, it was up to us to make something of the place and, by Jove,' he said, suddenly turning back to face her, 'That's just what we did.'

'You did?' Kit looked around uncertainly.

'Wasn't always in this mess, you know,' he said irritably. 'Time was when this costume museum was the jewel of the county. Place was humming with visitors from morning to night, six days a week, seven sometimes if we had a special do on.' The old man sighed. 'Hard to believe now.'

Kit was too polite to agree with him out loud, but inside she was incredulous. She just couldn't reconcile the museum's current state with Bard's description—Moonstone the jewel of the county, crammed with visitors? How could a place change that much?

'My missus, Katherine, was the boss,' said Bard, 'But we made a good team, her and me. She knew how to look after the costumes and I knew how to look after the gardens, plus I was a bit of a carpenter by trade, so you could say the job was made for the pair of us.'

'Right,' said Kit, a bit bewildered by the sudden change in her grandfather. His animation transformed him and she felt how different he must have been in the past.

'Well, there was plenty to keep us busy here when we first arrived. This place was in a heck of a muddle, ten times worse than it is now. People said we were daft to take it on, but they didn't know Katherine. Ooo, she had a way with her. Roll up her sleeves to anything, she would, and just about bursting with ideas for raising funds. She had sponsored walks and tea parties and costume lectures, and treasure hunts and training days. You won't believe it, but she even got up a play once.'

'A play? Really?'

'We did it alfresco, you know, in the gardens. Built a stage and everything. It was just over there on the lawn.' Bard turned eagerly to point, but the current overgrown state of the grounds seemed to strike him afresh and his arm dropped.

'So . . . er . . .' Kit hesitated. 'What went wrong?'

'What d'you mean?' he said, bristling up immediately.

Kit could have kicked herself for asking. Now they were back at square one again, with the old man morose and glum and her unable to think of the right thing to say.

Bard didn't seem to want to enter the museum while Finn Scudder was inside, so they hung around on the gravel, until long after opening time. Kit noticed that there was no sign of any other visitors. When Finn finally emerged through the front door, he was just as vile as he had been before.

Kit watched as he ostentatiously measured the front door, examined the condition of the walls and then took several hundred photographs of the most rotten looking windows. When he had finished, he strolled carelessly across to them.

'You two still here, then? What's the matter, had a family tiff or something?'

He turned for a last look at the building. 'You know, it's funny thing, but I remember the museum being bigger than that. What's happened to that room with all those flowery curtains?'

'What? Oh those, I took them down, for cleaning,' said Bard and Kit thought he looked a bit shifty.

'Well that'll be a first,' said Finn sarcastically. 'I'm pleased with the entrance hall though. The proportions are better than I remember. Of course, I'll have to replace those dodgy looking staircases and paint over all that gloomy wood panelling, but once I'm done, it'll make a first class reception area for the centre.'

'Centre?' repeated Kit blankly. 'What do you mean?'

'Conference centre of course. Hasn't your granddad told you? That's what this place will be in a year's time—Moonstone Conference Centre.'

Bard dug his hands deep in his pockets and kicked a stone.

'This part of the country is crying out for a new business resort. I've got investors coming out of my ears. Anyway, I'll be on my way now.' Finn raised his camera. 'I will of course be sharing my findings with the present owners.'

'What's that s'posed to mean?' growled Bard.

'Only that I thought I'd drop in on the council offices on my way home. They've turned a blind eye to what's been going on here for years because they didn't know what else to do. But that was before I came along offering to buy the place. They'd be crazy to turn me down. All I've got to do is show them what a dump Moonstone is and it'll be mine for the asking.' Finn waved his camera, tauntingly.

'You son of a maggot,' said Bard. 'You low down bit of dirt . . .' but he stopped because Kit had just caught hold of his arm and slipped her small hand into his. She had done it on impulse and wasn't sure if she was trying to comfort her grandfather or stop him doing something stupid. She held on tightly.

He stared down at his hand for a moment, before shaking her off angrily. By the time he was free, the property developer had already got into his car.

'By the way,' said Finn lowering the window. 'You've got some right old gargoyles in there haven't you?'

'Gargoyles?'

'Those prehistoric get-ups you've got standing around all over the place.'

'The mannequins?'

'That's it. Give me the creeps they do. There's one I spotted, had the biggest backside I ever saw. She looked like she had a chair under her skirt. Freaky looking thing and trailing bits of tatty old lace and God knows what all over the floor.'

'It's called a bustle,' said Bard stiffly. 'That's what women wore at the end of the nineteenth century.'

'Is it? I'll take your word for it, mate. Afraid I might have got a bit tangled up with all those frilly bits. Accident waiting to happen, really.'

He laughed, revved the engine provocatively and accelerated away in a shower of gravel.

As soon as the car was out of sight, Bard stormed into the museum and marched over to a gallery on the right. Kit scuttled along behind.

'I knew it,' he shouted. 'Look at the state of her. Accident waiting to happen indeed. If Finn Scudder didn't do that on purpose then I'll eat my hat.'

He was looking at a mannequin wearing a dress of rust-coloured silk. It had an eye wateringly large bottom and was undoubtedly the outfit that Finn had been talking about. The skirt had a long train and Kit could see clearly that the two bottom tiers of frills had been torn away from the hem of the garment.

'Oh dear,' said Kit. 'Is there anything you can do?'

'Course not. Drat the man.' Bard crouched

down painfully and began poking at the damage with a blunt finger, trying to see if he could hide it in some way.

Kit winced, but didn't say anything. He must know what he was doing. She moved away to look at the rest of the room, which appeared to be a spectacularly dusty library. It was like something out of Sleeping Beauty—a room frozen in time. The shelves were loaded with cobwebby books and every piece of furniture was covered in dust.

There was one other costume in the room, worn by a dummy with old-fashioned glasses and an ugly grey gown and apron. Kit wondered if it was some kind of maid's outfit and, without thinking, she put out her hand and swept a finger down one of the sleeves.

'Oops!'

She stared at what she had done. Where her finger had travelled there was now a gash of warmer brown. The dress wasn't grey after all, it was just thick with dust.

Kit leaned closer and blew at the front of the bodice. The air instantly filled with choking clouds and the whole dress seemed to give an angry jiggle. Kit stepped back quickly, as if she'd been burned. What exactly had just happened?

She glanced behind to see if her grandfather

had noticed anything, but he was still on his knees attending to the damage.

'Er, is it OK if I go and look round the rest of museum?' she asked, suddenly wanting to get away from the room.

Bard grunted his assent and, with one last wary look at the costume, Kit made her escape.

CHAPTER 5

Back in the hall, Kit quickly climbed the nearest staircase to the balcony above. The rest of the museum opened off this central atrium to the right and left in a series of connected apartments, and she set off to explore.

It was oddly silent. There were no other visitors and her footsteps sounded much too loud in the house. She found that she was tiptoeing, wanting to keep as quiet as she could, as if she was frightened of disturbing someone.

At first, what interested her most was the resemblance the museum had to her doll's house. Not every room had been reproduced in miniature. It seemed that whoever had made the replica had selected only a few of the best apartments to copy. It was fun tracking them down, and she was able to find matches for each one except the flowery wallpaper room that featured in her nightmare. Kit wasn't sure if she was relieved about this or disappointed.

There was something else odd about Moonstone. For a costume museum, there seemed to be very few garments on display. The best ones were downstairs in the oriental room, but upstairs they were few and far between. Kit occasionally came across one or two, lurking in the larger galleries, looking isolated and awkward. It was as if they had been dumped there by accident, and they never failed to give her a fright. They looked so lifelike. She approached them with caution, just in case . . . in case of what exactly?

Beside each one there was a small rickety sign on a stand, with a brief description of the outfit. Some of them had fallen over and Kit longed to pick them up, but she didn't dare in case Bard would consider this meddling. She paused to read the labels beside a couple of costumes. One was an American riding habit made out of green wool. The other, a black silk mourning gown from Australia, with a huge skirt and wide sleeves. Both were from the nineteenth century and had been acquired by someone called Rollo

Silk-Hatton.

There were other objects on display in the museum as well as costumes. One of the smaller galleries housed a large collection of bizarre looking musical instruments. Another was full of clocks. Then there was a room that contained a titanic-sized four poster bed. Kit had never seen anything like it. It could probably have slept about six people at once, and must have been constructed within the apartment itself as there was no way it could have come through the door. She read the label and discovered that it had been installed at Moonstone by Marmaduke Silk-Hatton in 1720.

But the weirdest gallery of all was the one full of walking sticks. Rollo Silk-Hatton must have been a big fan. There were literally hundreds of them, collected from all over the world. They were hung on the walls, suspended from the ceiling and arranged in large bins like flowers in a vase.

Kit noticed that one of the tubs was partially hiding a closed door. She looked at it with interest. Maybe this was the entrance to the flowery wallpaper room? She checked to make sure that no one was watching and tried the handle. Locked. Suddenly she became aware of an unpleasant burnt smell and, at the same moment, something caught her eye. On the floor was a little soft heap of cream fabric. She squatted down and scooped it up. It was light as air, a delicate, diaphanous scarf with a scalloped edge that belonged to another century. Kit thought she recognized it. Hadn't that girl dummy she had seen in the oriental room last night been wearing something like this?

She turned away from the locked door and got the fright of her life, because on the far side of the room, tucked behind yet another display of walking sticks, was the very mannequin she had just been thinking of. There was no doubt about it. Kit recognized the girl's sorrowful face and her mushroom-coloured gown. Then she noticed something else. Her scarf was missing.

Kit couldn't move. What on earth was going on? How had the costume got there? The only possible explanation was that Bard had done it. But why would he have gone to the trouble of lugging the dummy all the way up here and then cramming it in behind a bucket of walking sticks?

Just then, a slight sound clipped the air and one of the walking sticks shifted slightly in a bucket. Kit spun round in alarm, then, with the scarf still clutched tightly in her hand, she got out of the room as fast as she could. Maybe she'd done enough exploring for one day.

She hurried back to the hall and pushed open the door that led to her grandfather's flat. She was in such a rush that she was halfway up the stairs before she realized that she had made a mistake. She stopped outside a door labelled 'Costume Store'. This wasn't the right staircase, it was spiral. She must have gone the wrong way.

Maybe if she carried on going up, it would lead back to the flat anyway. So she set off again. There was a fusty, peppery smell of old, dry paper and the steps corkscrewed steeply upwards. At the top she emerged, head first, into a large attic. Kit looked around and immediately forgot about everything else.

She was looking at the last thing she expected. It was some kind of a sewing room. Her neck prickled with excitement as she climbed up the last few steps. What would she give for a place like this? Think of all the making she could do up here. There was everything she needed—an entire chest stuffed with scissors, tape measures, paintbrushes, fabrics, and threads. There were tools she had never even seen before and a vast and wonderful table.

On it was an old, yellowing sewing machine

with a pincushion, iced with dust like a cupcake. This must have been where her grandmother, Katherine had repaired the costumes long ago. Kit pulled up a stool and sat down. She drew a smile in the dust on the table. Maybe her mum had sat in this very spot when she was a girl and learned how to sew. As if to confirm this idea, Kit suddenly noticed a pair of tweezers laid on the table next to the machine. They were identical to the pair Kit had so recently been using, from her mother's sewing box.

* * *

Later on that morning, Kit unpacked her bag in her bedroom. She had no idea how long she would be staying at Moonstone, but there was no harm in making herself at home while she was here.

She put her clothes away in the chest, pulling wide the hollow, rattling drawers one after the other. They released a powerful smell of aged wood into the air and Kit wondered how long it had been since anyone had opened them. She still had the scarf she had found in the gallery and, not knowing what else to do with it, she slipped it into the top drawer for safe keeping.

'Oi! grub!' barked a voice from the bottom of

the stairs.

Kit jumped guiltily and hurried down to join her grandfather in the kitchen.

Eating together was awkward and uncomfortable. Bard must have used up his word count for the day on his little outburst that morning, and munched his way through a plate of cheese on toast, without even looking at her. Every subject seemed to be off limits and if Kit did try to make small talk, she usually said the wrong thing, like when she enquired if Moonstone had been busy that morning.

'Don't talk daft,' snapped the old man and that was the end of any lunchtime conversation.

During the evening meal, Kit had another go. In between mouthfuls of beans on toast, she forced herself to ask him some more questions. His answers continued to be terse and discouraging but she persisted, and in this way she scraped together a few basic facts about Moonstone. It seemed that although the museum was open daily, there were generally very few visitors, and that Bard spent most of his time hanging around in the hall waiting for them to come. It sounded pretty awful to Kit.

'Er, I liked the room with the walking sticks in,' she said cautiously. 'Do you ever put costumes in there?'

'Course not,' said Bard.

'Never?'

The old man stirred his tea irritably and didn't bother to answer.

'Is there another gallery beyond it?' Kit persevered.

'What?' snapped Bard. 'No!'

'Oh,' said Kit, 'So where does that other door lead?'

'Nowhere. It's a broom cupboard, that's all.'

Kit gave up, and after washing-up the plates, said she would go to bed early.

'Go steady with the hot water in the bathroom,' said Bard, which Kit interpreted as his way of saying goodnight.

* * *

After what had happened last night, Kit felt tense and uneasy as she got into bed. She was tempted to leave the light on, but thought that Bard might not approve, so she contented herself with pulling the lamp closer, so that it was within easy reach. Then she lay down under the covers with her eyes screwed tightly shut, listening out for any unusual sounds.

Nothing happened, and the minutes ticked slowly by. Despite her concerns, Kit began to feel drowsy and finally dropped off.

And it happened all over again just as before. Kit woke suddenly in the dark, heart pounding, convinced there was someone in her room.

'Who's there?'

There was silence and nothing moved. Downstairs the clock started striking the hour. She counted the chimes. Midnight.

Remembering the lamp, she stretched out a trembling hand, and found the switch.

PING—the light went on.

Kit's eyes flew round the room, searching, but there was nothing there. She pulled the blankets up round her neck to keep warm. Time passed. Her mind began to wander over the happenings of the day. She thought about the costumes she had seen in the museum; the rust-coloured bustle that Finn Scudder had trodden on. The riding habit and mourning gown from the nineteenth century, and the sad looking girl in the mushroom-coloured gown, penned in behind the walking sticks. How had she got there?

Out of the corner of her eye, Kit thought she saw her bedroom curtains twitch. Instantly she was sitting bolt upright, the adrenalin pumping. Had she imagined it, or was there something actually behind them? There was only one way to find out. She pushed back the covers and cautiously tiptoed across the room. It took her a moment to find the courage to do what she had to, but at last she reached for the curtain and swept it back. Then she clamped a hand over her mouth to stop herself screaming.

CHAPTER 6

There, cowering back against the window, was
the girl in the mushroom-coloured gown. But
no longer was she a lifeless mannequin. She was
trembling as much as Kit. Without warning she
gathered her petticoat in her hands, ran for the
door and disappeared from sight down the attic
stairs.

Kit felt as though she couldn't breathe
properly, as if she had just been thumped. She
stumbled to the door and listened, but she could
hear nothing except the sound of the clock
ticking and the faint rumble of her grandfather's
snores.

What should she do? Wake Bard and tell
him? But that was unthinkable. Still breathless

and shaky, Kit found herself beside the chest, pulling open the top drawer. She grabbed the cream shawl and headed back to the door. She had never felt so frightened in her life, but she had to find out what was going on.

She crept out of her room, placing her bare feet with care on the splintery old boards. Reaching the door to the flat, she eased it open, slipped out into the main building and closed it softly behind her.

Now she could move more easily, but she was also alone in the darkness, without even the comfort of the old man's snores. She could only see where she was going because the moon had come out and was giving off a faint ghostly light through the windows. As she tiptoed down the stairs that led to the museum, she noticed a change. There was a warm glow up ahead. Someone had switched the lights on, and Kit was pretty sure that it wasn't Bard.

She reached the bottom, pushed the door open, and stepped out into the light. Then she stopped dead because just in front of her, looking over the balcony that circled the hall, was the girl in the mushroom-coloured gown.

Kit didn't move, and for a moment neither did the girl. She had her back to Kit and was obviously unaware that anyone was there. She must have sensed something though, because suddenly she swung round and they were facing each other.

The girl looked terrified and Kit had to act fast. She thrust the scarf forward, unfolding it and holding it out in front of her like a peace offering. Slowly, step by step Kit approached, until they were in touching distance. The scarf trembled between them and then, in one swift movement, the girl reached out and took it.

Once she had it safe, she threw the wrap around her shoulders and expertly tucked the ends into the front of her gown. She considered Kit warily for a moment, but then a wonderful thing happened. She smiled and her strained little face filled with warmth. Kit smiled back and the girl beckoned. She turned towards the rail and it was clear that she was inviting Kit to join her. Side by side they stood together and when the girl looked down into the hall, Kit followed suit.

It was as if the floor had suddenly tilted under her feet. Kit grasped the banister for support. She felt dazed with shock because, down below, the hall was not empty and silent as it should have been, it was teeming with hundreds of historic costumes. The mannequins in the museum had come to life.

They were sauntering around arm in arm,
talking to each other, bowing and curtsying.
It was like watching the opening scene of an
unknown play, Kit half expected the figures to
suddenly break into song or start dancing.

The variety of outfits was enormous; different
colours, different shapes, different periods,
different cultures. There were examples from
all over the world. They gathered together
in groups and Kit's eyes darted from one to
the next. On her left, she could see a Native
American woman deep in conversation with
a lady in a blue and white stripy gown, while
on her right, a couple of gentlemen in historic
dressing gowns were strolling alongside what
looked like a male Inuit. Meanwhile, in the
centre of the room, there was a particularly
eccentric looking collection, made up of a vicar
in a church vestment, a woman in a stunning red
and gold sari, an African warrior and a dancer
in a ballet tutu, who kept pointing her toe and
attempting to balance on one leg.

Just then, a suit of armour appeared and
clanked across the hall. The crowd below shifted
and moved to let him pass, and it seemed to Kit
that amongst all this diversity, there was only
one thing missing—there were no children. She
looked sideways at the girl next to her, maybe

this was why she seemed so sad.

Kit was surprised by how few of the costumes she actually recognized. Every now and then she spotted one that she'd seen on display in the galleries, but the majority were completely new to her. She wondered where they had all come from. Then, with a twinge of concern, she observed what bad condition they were all in. Holes, stains, splits, and dirt. There seemed to be something wrong with every garment.

Kit noticed something else too. It wasn't all friendliness amongst the costumes. There were some filthy looks being thrown around. A man in a Chinese dragon robe and a woman dressed in acid yellow appeared to be particularly unpopular, but the feeling was obviously mutual. They kept themselves to themselves and, when a lady wearing voluminous bloomers entered the hall pushing a bicycle, they drew back in horror as if there was something unseemly about her.

As Kit watched, snatches of conversations floated up to her. If only she could hear them more clearly. She could see the lady in the rust-coloured bustle that Finn Scudder had damaged, who looked as though she was telling her woes to a man in a military uniform. Kit leaned over, straining to catch her words.

'Such a terrible shock . . . my train will never

be the same again . . . I'll be moved to the store now, you mark my words.'

She moved away, trailing her torn lace behind, and now there was a woman in a Russian outfit just below talking to the lady in the black mourning gown that Kit had seen earlier that day. The only words that reached the balcony were frustratingly broken up.

'A search party for little Minna . . . Both of them I hear, Lady Ann Hoops and Kiko Kai . . . mustn't give up?'

Was that someone crying? Yes, down below, the lady in the mourning gown had a scrap of hankie in her hand and was dabbing her eyes and sniffing.

'He frightens me so,' she sobbed. 'Captain John flung his long sleeves right in my face . . . He's dotty as a plum pudding.'

With these words still lingering in her ears, Kit suddenly looked round, aware of a slight disturbance beside her. The girl in the mushroom-coloured gown was backing away in alarm, her eyes fixed on something further along the balcony. Kit twisted round to see what it was, and jumped.

Not far away, there was a figure standing in the shadows. It was the man in the long white robe that she had spotted in the oriental room on her first night at Moonstone. He swung a pair of elongated sleeves from side to side and he was staring straight at her. Kit knew instantly that this must be the very Captain John that the lady in the black dress had just been crying about.

'Hey!' he yelled, suddenly pointing at her with one of his long, dangling sleeves. 'Was it you who locked the door to the portrait gallery?'

Kit took a step backwards, her heart rate picking up speed again.

'How dare you and Fenella play such a trick on me? Plotted it together, did you? Thought it was funny?'

Kit shook her head uncertainly. 'Umm . . . I don't know what you mean.'

'Codswallop!'

Kit glanced at the girl beside her, she looked even more terrified, so Kit spoke up bravely. 'I think you've made a mistake, sir. We haven't been plotting anything together. We've only just met. I didn't even know her name until you said it.'

'HA!' cried Captain John, advancing towards them so that Kit and Fenella had to step backwards again. 'Do you expect me to believe that? You will unlock the door for me immediately, IMMEDIATELY, DO YOU

HEAR!'

Kit looked in panic at Fenella again. Surely it was her turn to say something. After all, she must know more about this crazy captain than Kit did. But the girl remained silent and all they could do was carry on walking backwards. Soon they were reversing side by side into the gallery of clocks and then through the room of musical instruments, and, all the time, Captain John was following them and getting angrier by the second.

At last they were entering the gallery with the walking sticks, and Kit became suddenly aware that they were heading straight for a dead end.

'THERE IT IS!' bawled the Captain at the top of his voice and Kit nearly fell over with the shock. Fenella looked like she was about to pass out. The man was flapping both his sleeves violently in the direction of the locked door. Why on earth did he want to get in there? Bard had said there was nothing beyond but a broom cupboard.

Fenella pushed a tub of walking sticks to one side and together they backed against the door. They were trapped. What on earth were they going to do now? The Captain was coming nearer every second and on impulse, Kit seized a stick from the bucket beside her and waved it threateningly at him.

'Look I don't know what your problem is, but we didn't lock this door,' she shouted.

And just like that, the man stopped. His sleeves became still and his face changed. All the anger in him evaporated and he eyed the stick in Kit's hand with sudden interest.

'Ahh, yes indeed,' he said, his voice sounding disconcertingly good-humoured. 'My Malacca cane. I mislaid it somewhere, did I not? How very kind of you to return it to me.'

Completely bewildered, Kit let him tug the stick out of her hand and examine it.

'But this is not mine.'

'Er . . . isn't it?' said Kit.

'No, mine has a silver top.' He handed it back to her.

'Right,' said Kit. Then she had a brainwave. 'Well, there are loads of other sticks here to choose from, why don't you borrow one until you find your own?'

The Captain seemed to approve of this idea and was soon rummaging in a bucket of sticks, pulling out one after another and striking a pose with each.

'What do you think of this one? Not bad, eh? Perhaps a trifle heavy? I like to be able to

87

swing 'um as I walk along.' The Captain was so absorbed in what he was doing that he didn't notice Kit and Fenella tiptoeing past.

They were nearly out of the gallery before he realized what was going on, and then his former frenzy returned in full force. He was instantly back in pursuit.

'Stop! Come back, you young devils . . .'

But this time they didn't hang around. Fenella grabbed Kit's hand and they ran for it. Looking back, Kit could see Captain John charging after them. Fortunately, he was slightly hampered by the armful of walking sticks he was still holding, and this gave them the advantage.

The girls galloped back through the galleries, then hurtled around the balcony that skirted the hall and up the passage towards Bard's flat. Not caring how much noise she made, Kit raced up the stairs to her bedroom and flung open the door. But when she looked back, Fenella was gone.

She hesitated in the doorway, peering out and listening. But there was complete silence. Still breathing fast, Kit closed the door at last and slumped onto the floor with her back against it, clutching the walking stick to her chest.

CHAPTER 7

Kit woke up in daylight feeling cold and stiff. She sat up gingerly. Every part of her seemed to be aching. She looked around. What was she doing on her bedroom floor? Lying next to her on the ground was a walking stick. Suddenly Kit was wide awake and everything came flooding back; all those museum mannequins wearing costumes, alive and moving and being chased by that crazy man with the flailing sleeves, and Fenella grabbing her hand and racing with her through the galleries.

Questions swarmed in her brain. What had happened afterwards? Was everything back to normal now?

Most of all she thought about Fenella. She

remembered how strangely silent the girl had been and the haunting sadness that hung about her. But there had been that one moment when she'd smiled and she had looked happy then.

Kit wondered anxiously where she had gone last night, praying that she hadn't been caught by the Captain. She had a sudden vision of him, dragging Fenella back to the locked door, yelling at her to open it. Why was the man so fixated on getting into a broom cupboard? Unless it wasn't a cupboard, and Bard had made that up.

Kit had an idea. She stood up and moved over to the bed. On the wall above it was the map of the museum that her mum had drawn. She knelt on her pillow, so she could see it better.

It took her a moment to get her bearings. The map was beautifully drawn. Her mum had marked in every fireplace, door and window in the museum and each gallery was labelled with a name. Kit wondered if she had made them up. There was one called 'the boudoir'—that must be the four poster bedroom—and 'the cogs' was obviously the clock gallery. Further along was 'the music salon', followed by the walking-stick gallery, which was labelled 'the rabology room'. Kit placed a finger on the map and stared. This was where Bard's broom cupboard should have been, only it wasn't. According to her mum, there were two more apartments beyond the locked door—'the portrait gallery' and 'the summer room'.

'Bard,' said Kit, bursting into the kitchen a moment later with the framed drawing in her hand. 'Why did you tell me that there was a cupboard behind that locked door in the walking-stick room? It's not true. There are two more galleries. I can see them on my mum's map.'

The old man was standing at the sink with his back to her. 'What's that?' he said without looking round.

'On my mum's map, there are two more galleries beyond that locked door. Why did you tell me it was just a cupboard?'

'Oh, did I? Er . . . must have been thinking of somewhere else,' said Bard, still fiddling with something at the sink. Kit thought this was pretty lame and didn't believe him for one minute.

'Why are the galleries shut? Can I see inside?'

'No,' said Bard shortly, leaning further over the sink.

'It wouldn't take long. I just want to see if there is anything . . . anything of interest there.' She was thinking of the Captain.

'I said NO!' shouted her grandfather and

slammed both hands down on the draining board.

Kit was silenced immediately, but there was no time to feel guilty because at that moment Bard turned round.

'Wow,' said Kit, disconcerted. 'You look . . . different. Are you going somewhere?'

The old man was wearing a jacket and tie and he had obviously been trying to clean the mud off his old boots.

'Axly,' said Bard shortly. 'Got some business on.'

'Oh.'

'You'll have to stop here on your own for a couple of hours. You can keep an eye on the museum for me.'

'I can't do that,' said Kit in a panic. 'Don't leave me here on my own. What if . . . what if something happens?'

'You expecting a bus load of trippers or something?' said Bard sarcastically. 'Don't trouble yourself. Public never come when it's raining.'

But it wasn't the public Kit was worrying about.

'I had a phone call from the council earlier,' explained the old man, sitting down on a chair and slowly pulling on his boots. 'Someone's made a formal complaint about the museum. Three guesses who that'll be.'

'Finn Scudder,' breathed Kit.

'I've been asked to come in for a meeting. Apparently they want to talk to me in person, whatever that means.'

Kit didn't like the sound of this and watched the old man as he straightened up painfully. 'Anyway, thought I'd better tidy myself up a bit for the occasion. How do I look?'

Kit blinked. Bard's shirt was crumpled and dirty, the jacket was old and frayed, and the tie clashed horribly with both. She thought about the rails of crisply laundered shirts and smart suits in her dad's cupboard at home and a lump came into her throat.

'You look . . . you look really smart,' said Kit.

Bard snorted. 'Not much of a liar, are you? Tell you what, I'll put the closed sign on the door while I'm gone. That'll stop you fretting.'

She was touched by this consideration, even though locking the door wasn't going to make her feel any safer.

* * *

With her grandfather gone, Kit stood in the kitchen listening. The clock ticked loudly, but behind it there was a brooding silence. Without planning to, she found herself creeping down the passage to the museum, and was soon wandering through the galleries. She felt jumpy and on edge, and kept looking over her shoulder to see if anyone was there.

The first figure she came to was the one wearing the black mourning gown, who Kit had seen crying last night. The wisp of hanky was still tucked into her hand, but the fingers that held it were lifeless and cold. It was nothing but a faded dress on an old cracked mannequin.

Kit turned away and moved on, passing through room after room, inspecting the outfits that were on display. But there was no spark of life in any of them. She tried waving in their faces, shouting at them, but nothing happened. And the more she looked, the more perplexed she became, because there seemed to be so few of them. Where were all the other costumes that she'd seen yesterday? That girl with the bicycle, the Inuit man, the ballet dancer? There had been loads of them in the hall.

And it wasn't only this that was bothering Kit. She couldn't find Fenella either. There was no sign of her behind the walking sticks in the rabology room, and nor was she downstairs behind the screen where Kit had first spotted her.

* * *

Bard returned three hours later. She heard the
sound of the Land Rover with relief and ran
downstairs to meet him. He came through the
front door, looking furious, dumped a couple
of heavy shopping bags on the floor and then
disappeared into the library.

Feeling uneasy, she followed him inside and
found him having another look at the damage
that Finn Scudder had caused yesterday.

'Blasted man,' muttered Bard, glaring at the
tattered train.

Kit hovered nervously. She could tell that the
meeting had not gone well.

'Was it Finn Scudder that made the
complaint, then?' she asked hesitantly.

Bard went to a cupboard and took out a dirty
dust sheet. 'According to the council, they're not
authorized to say, but course it was.'

'What happened?' asked Kit.

'There's going to be a formal enquiry.'

'What does that mean?'

'Apparently they're going to consider how
to proceed and then let me know soon, but I'm
guessing they'll want to come and have a good

poke around Moonstone.'

'And then?'

Bard shrugged and handed her the dust sheet. 'Unfold that will you. Might as well make yourself useful.'

'What are you doing?'

'Got to get this old bustle off display, haven't I.'

'Why?'

'Well look at the state of her, can't leave the old girl in here looking like that. Lay the dust sheet down next to her and we'll shift her up to the store.'

Kit silently obeyed, but as she helped Bard drag the costume out into the hall, she couldn't help worrying what the lady in the bustle would think about being moved like this.

Then began the awful process of carrying her upstairs.

'Sorry,' said Kit for the tenth time, as the dummy knocked awkwardly against the last step.

'Who are you talking too?' puffed Bard. 'Sounds like you're apologizing to the blasted mannequin.'

Kit changed the subject quickly. 'Where are we going?'

He pointed towards the spiral stairs that

led up to the sewing room. Kit thought he was joking. Then she suddenly remembered the door labelled Costume Store that she'd passed yesterday and realized that he wasn't.

It was a horrible job. The spiral stairs were impossibly narrow and the bustle kept getting jammed. They made it at last and Bard pushed the door open, hauling the figure inside.

Kit stood in the entrance, stunned. The place was literally crammed with mannequins in historic dress. They were squashed up against each other, their fragile silks and satins crushed. This was not simply a store, it was a graveyard.

At least it solved one mystery. Now Kit knew where all the missing costumes were.

'Wow,' she said, pointing at a gown she had never seen before. 'Is that for real?'

'Oh, that old mantua,' said Bard. 'Bit of a sight, isn't she? They wore them at European courts in the eighteenth century, to show off their fine fabrics.'

The costume was made out of ivory silk and though it was dirty, it was beautifully decorated with embroidered flowers. But it was the size of the thing that amazed Kit. The skirt stuck out at the sides so far that it looked as if there was an actual table hidden underneath. Kit couldn't imagine how Bard had got it up here.

She turned towards him now and watched as he attempted to jam the bustle into a tiny space. There was a horrible tearing noise as he twisted the mannequin round.

'Bard, stop,' said Kit in desperation. 'You're making it worse. There must be something else we can do? Can't we try and mend her or something?'

'Mend her?' said Bard. 'Don't be daft. Even if we knew how to sew, we couldn't do much. Fixing old garments like these is specialist work. Takes years to learn how to do it.'

'Does it?'

'My wife Katherine was an expert and then she trained up Emmie.'

'My mum looked after the costumes?' This was a revelation to Kit.

'She was a complete natural with a needle,' said Bard. 'Katherine always said that the fairies must have taught her how to sew. She could make anything. When Katherine died. Emmie had to take over all her mum's work in the museum. She was only young, but she loved the costumes like they were people. Then she gave it up to marry your dad. Proper waste it was to throw all that away.'

Kit silently agreed.

'Anyway, once she went, there was no one left

here to look after the costumes. Council didn't want to know, of course, and when they started falling to bits, all I could do was hide them up here in this store. I can't even thread a needle.'

Bard sounded bitter and ashamed and Kit didn't know what to say. She was beginning to understand what the old man had been up against; stranded here alone, without any support from the local authority. No wonder the costumes were in such a mess. If only she could learn how to look after them, like her mum and grandmother. But who was there at Moonstone to teach her now?

CHAPTER 8

'I wouldn't say no to eating that again,' said
Bard as he wiped up the last bit of bolognese
with a crust of toast and posted it in his mouth.

Kit had offered to cook for him on her first
day at Moonstone and he'd surprised her greatly
by bringing back the ingredients for spaghetti
bolognese from Axly.

'It's better with pasta,' said Kit. This was the
only thing that he had forgotten to buy.

'Nothing wrong with having it on toast.
Makes a nice change.'

Kit wasn't sure if he was joking. At least the
meal had put him in a better mood.

'You're not going to bed yet,' said Kit
grabbing his arm as Bard rose to his feet. She

was feeling increasingly nervous as night approached.

'Seeing to the dishes is all. What's got you so jumpy?'

'I'm not jumpy,' said Kit. 'Only I was wondering . . . Do you know if . . . I mean, have you ever been disturbed here at night before?'

'What?'

'You know, by unexplained noises or something.'

Bard stopped scraping out the pan and stared at her. 'You're never asking me if Moonstone is haunted?'

'Not exactly haunted,' said Kit and then stopped. There was no way she could tell Bard what was really on her mind.

'Did my mum ever worry about ghosts when she was young?'

Bard snorted. 'Not her. She never thought twice about wandering around the museum in the middle of the night. Couldn't get her to go to bed.'

'Really?'

'Now you listen to me, Kit—I've lived here for decades now and I've never heard anything yet that made me think Moonstone was haunted.'

'That's good,' said Kit. 'I'm probably just imagining stuff.'

'Course you are. Mind you,' added Bard unhelpfully, 'I've never met another being who sleeps as deep as I do. A bomb could go off in the room and I wouldn't wake.'

They finished the washing-up and after that there was nothing for Kit to do but go up to bed. She cleaned her teeth and put on her pyjamas, but she didn't think there was much chance she would actually sleep. All she could think about was the costumes. Would they would come to life again?

Time was edging relentlessly closer to midnight.

Kit tried to persuade herself that the last thing she wanted to do was go out into the museum in the dark. It was madness even to consider it. That crazy captain might be on the loose again. But then she thought of Fenella. What if something really had happened to her? Was Kit too much of a coward to check that she was all right?

The clock downstairs chimed midnight at last and Kit scrambled out of bed.

* * *

Down in the great hall, the lights were on again. Kit could see the glow coming through the door at the bottom of the stairs. This time she was much more cautious about venturing out onto the balcony and checked first that the coast was clear. To her relief, there was no sign of Captain John, but Fenella was also absent and she felt a twinge of anxiety for her.

As she stood in the doorway, she became conscious of a commotion going on down below, a rumble of many people talking. Suddenly a harsh aristocratic voice rang out loudly over the top.

'Will all ladies and gentleman from the eighteenth century make their way over here please.Beatrice Bligh, what are you doing dithering about in the middle? You really ought to know which century you belong to by now.'

On hands and knees, Kit crawled to the railings and looked down into the hall. There were even more costumes present tonight, but unlike yesterday they weren't milling around in the same free and easy way. It looked as if there was some kind of event going on, and everyone was positioning themselves deliberately on one side of the room or the other with a definite division down the middle. Most of them had now shuffled into place, except for one lady in a high wasted dress, who didn't seem to know where to go.

'Beatrice, for heaven's sake, pull yourself together,' barked the aristocratic voice, and Kit saw that it belonged to the lady wearing the table-sized mantua she had seen in the store earlier. 'I refuse to go through this all over again. How many times do I have to tell you, your fabric is from the eighteenth century, therefore your place is with us.' And, grabbing Beatrice by the hand, she tried to pull her over to her side of the room.

The attempt was foiled by the woman in the Japanese kimono from the oriental room, who glided out of the crowd and grasped Beatrice's other hand, tugging in the opposite direction.

'Be that as it may, Lady Ann Hoops,' she said in a deep, silky voice that contrasted strongly with the harsh tones of her opponent, 'but her gown was made at the beginning of the nineteenth century, which means she belongs with me.'

'I cannot agree, Kiko Kia. The material that a costume is made from is integral to its identity. We have always considered Beatrice as one of us, and one of us she will remain.'

'But I think you will find that dear Beatrice feels much more at home amongst costumes from the nineteenth century. Perhaps we should leave it up to her to decide?'

Beatrice looked panic-stricken at the thought of having to choose between two such fearsome rivals. Luckily for her, Lady Ann decided to trade this battle in for another.

'Well, if you're having Beatrice, I want first choice on which part of the museum the eighteenth century will search tonight.'

Kiko bowed her head graciously. She had a peculiarly slow and exaggerated way of moving, as if she was determined that everything she did should be elegant and dignified.

'We'll take upstairs,' said Lady Ann immediately.

'But surely, that is where you looked last time, and if I remember rightly, you failed to find anything.'

'No more than the nineteenth century failed the time before that,' snapped Lady Ann.

Kiko paused to consider her next move. 'If you can assure me, Lady Ann, that none of my people will be troubled by Captain John during tonight's search, then I am happy to agree to anything.'

Lady Ann pursed her lips and inhaled sharply through pinched nostrils.

'I don't know what you're talking about. The Captain is perfectly harmless, he's just been a trifle confused of late.'

'The man has become a liability. Why, only last night he threw a bundle of walking sticks at Claudia. She was in great distress about it.'

'Well, Claudia Clack is a ninny,' said Lady Ann. 'She's never happy unless she's got something to cry about.'

Kit glanced curiously round the hall to see what everyone else was making of this argument. The costumes looked fairly resigned and Kit got the impression that they were used to this kind of bickering. Over on the nineteenth-century side of the room, the ballet costume was practicing her pliés, using one of the gentlemen in a dressing gown as a barre, while the lady with the voluminous bloomers was absentmindedly tinging the bell of her bicycle.

Meanwhile, in the eighteenth-century camp, a gent in an elaborate suit of duck-egg blue was playing cards with the man in the Chinese dragon robe. Kit thought she could see a splash of mushroom-coloured silk behind them and wondered if it was Fenella. She edged further around the banister to try and get a better view.

'I say,' said someone. 'Who's that up there?'

It was the man in the suit who had been playing cards. His words carried clearly across the big hall and Kit froze behind the rail. Was he talking about at her?

'I beg your pardon, Sir Jasper,' said Lady Ann, frowning at the interruption.

'Up there, in the gallery. There's a young lad watching us.'

Lady Ann turned round to look and at the same moment, everyone in the hall followed suit.

'Good gracious me, Sir Jasper Stockings is right,' said Lady Ann. She glared ferociously up at Kit. 'You there! What is the meaning of this? How dare you spy on us in this fashion? Come down here and explain yourself.'

Kit rose slowly from the floor. Her legs were wobbling so much that she had to hang onto the rail to keep herself upright. A sea of hostile faces were staring up at her, and if it hadn't been for the fact that she had just spotted Fenella in the crowd, she would probably have run away. Fenella lifted one hand and gave her the tiniest of waves.

Fractionally reassured, Kit began the awful descent down the stairs. She felt horribly conspicuous. Every eye in the hall was on her and the silence made her feel loud and clumsy. When she reached the bottom, the crowd drew apart to let her pass, then closed in again behind her. There was no escape now.

In the centre of the room, Kit halted in

front of the two formidable women. Close up
Lady Ann Hoops and Kiko Kai were even more
terrifying than they had been from a distance.
The haughty expression of one, coupled with
the disdainful stare of the other, was enough to
make anyone quake.

'Gadzooks,' murmured Sir Jasper from just
behind them. 'Look at those stripy long johns
he's wearing. Never seen anything like 'um.
Where d'you come from, boy?'

'I'm . . . I'm . . . Actually, I'm a girl,' said Kit.

'A girl? Dear me!' exclaimed Lady Ann.
'Whatever made you cut off your hair like that?
Have you been ill? What century are you from?'

Kit glanced nervously around for Fenella. She
had a feeling that this wasn't going to go down
terribly well. 'The t . . . twenty-first century.'

There was a horrified gasp from all the
costumes followed by an outbreak of muttering.
Just then, Kit felt a touch on her hand and saw
with relief that Fenella was beside her.

'Well, if that is the case,' said Lady Ann
Hoops. 'You had better join Kiko Kai's search
party.'

'Why mine?' said Kiko her voice rising
indignantly.

'Obviously because the child is closer to you
in age.'

'Oh, is she indeed! Well if that's the case then I am sure you won't mind inviting Giles Clanker to be one of your party.'

'Giles Clanker is dressed in a sixteenth-century suit of armour, not a costume,' said Lady Ann contemptuously. 'Anyway, he's not the joining-in type.'

It looked like another long and pointless argument was underway. Luckily Sir Jasper broke in with a suggestion.

'I don't mind taking charge of the lad. He can come along with me and Fenella.'

This was grudgingly agreed to by Lady Ann, and Kit found herself climbing back up the stairs with all the mannequins in eighteenth-century costumes, jammed in between her friend and Sir Jasper Stockings. She had no idea what she was meant to be doing. As far as she could tell, she was taking part in some kind of a search party.

'Who are we hunting for?' she whispered to Fenella, who was suddenly looking strained. She didn't answer and it was Sir Jasper who replied.

'Minna, of course,' he said. 'Dear little thing. Great admirer of the game hide-and-go-seek.'

'Do you mean she's a child?' said Kit. 'How long has she been missing?'

'Who knows,' said Sir Jasper vaguely. 'Some time I should say.' They reached the top of the stairs.

'Let's start in the west wing, shall we?' he suggested. 'Don't want to go anywhere near the privies. Between you and me, I've locked Captain John in there to keep him out of the way. Gave him a pile of walking sticks and left him happy as Larry building wigwams and booby traps.' Sir Jasper sighed. 'Heaven knows what we're to do with the man. I don't like to agree with Kiko Kai, but he's getting worse every day.'

'Did . . . did something happen to make him go funny?' asked Kit.

'He's been this way ever since he got locked out of the portrait gallery. It's rather unhinged his mind, poor fellow. Awkward business. Lady Ann is at her wits' end and Kiko Kai never misses a chance to stick the knife in. It's made them detest each other worse than ever, and that has a bad effect on everyone. Never known the place at such sixes and sevens. And what with Minna missing and Fenella so down in the dumps, Moonstone is about as happy as a mortuary at the moment.'

Sir Jasper looked troubled and Fenella stroked his sleeve apologetically.

'Would it help if I could find a way to open the portrait gallery?' asked Kit cautiously.

Sir Jasper brightened. 'Rather,' he said. 'If we

could only get that devilish door unlocked, I'm certain Captain John would be back to his old self in no time.'

'Well I suppose I could try,' said Kit, wondering uneasily how this would be possible without involving Bard.

Just then, Giles Clanker stomped past, his armoured plates jangling loudly. Kit leaped out of his way and flattened herself against the wall. She was just a tiny bit afraid of Giles in his suit of armour.

The next few hours were spent scouring the upstairs galleries with Fenella, looking for the mysterious Minna. Together they searched inside cupboards and chests, behind tapestries and curtains, and throughout it all, Fenella never said a single word. Kit began to wonder if she could speak at all.

At first all the costumes in the museum were hunting too, but after an hour or so, most of them had given up. All except Fenella, who worked on with a dogged determination that Kit found slightly worrying.

Who was this Minna that Fenella was so anxious to find, and how could she have gone missing in the first place? Kit did her best to help, but she was so tired by this point that when Fenella entered a gallery they had already

scoured, and started searching behind the
curtains all over again, she put her foot down.

'We've looked here already. There's no point
doing it again,' she said, but her companion
ignored her and carried on, desperately pulling
back the dusty drapes. 'Fenella, please stop,' said
Kit. She grasped one of the girl's wrists but she
shook herself free angrily, walked a few steps
away and then seemed to crumple. She covered
her face in her hands and her shoulders shook.

Kit stared in dismay. There was obviously
far more to all of this than she had realized. She
didn't know what to say, so she put out her hand
and laid it tentatively on Fenella's shoulder,
feeling her silent sobs.

CHAPTER 9.

Kit stayed in bed late the following morning, and when she did finally come to she felt groggy and sick. Her few hours of sleep had been broken and restless and her old doll's house nightmare had woken her twice. She had only been staying at Moonstone for three nights, but she was conscious of how much worse the dream had got since she arrived. Her terror at being trapped in the room with the flowery wallpaper felt so real and the smell of smoke seemed to linger on even after she was awake.

She pulled on some clothes and stumbled downstairs, with her hair on end and her eyes sill gluey with sleep. There was no sign of Bard in the kitchen, but she found him a moment later, seated at a desk in his tiny office.

'Morning,' mumbled Kit through the door.

'You call this morning, do you?' said Bard. 'Practically dinner time.' He took off his glasses, huffed onto the lenses and attempted to rub them clean with the same filthy handkerchief Kit had seen him use before.

'What are you doing?'

'Admin,' he said, replacing his glasses. Then he grunted with frustration. 'Oh, I dunno, these don't seem any better, no matter how many times I clean 'um.'

'Let me try,' said Kit. She took the glasses to the kitchen and washed them thoroughly.

'S'pose that's a bit better,' said Bard grudgingly as he put the now gleaming glasses back on.

'So what's the admin?' asked Kit curiously.

'Accounts. Thought I'd better put them in order, case someone from the rotten old council comes snooping round. They could come any day, I suppose.'

Kit looked uncertainly at the pile of crumpled receipts in front of him. The notebook he was using looked like a museum piece in its own right.

'Maybe I can help,' said Kit. 'I'm not brilliant at maths like my brother and sister, but I've had a lot of extra coaching.'

'Best thing you can do is keep out of my way,' snapped Bard. 'Reckon I'm better at bookkeeping than a twelve-year-old nipper like you.'

Kit didn't say anything, but observing the way Bard was now rotating one of the receipts as if he didn't know which way up it went, she wasn't sure this was true. She couldn't bear to watch and glanced around the office instead. It was small and chaotic, with piles of dusty folders and newspapers all over the floor. There wasn't much furniture, just a desk, filing cabinet and a small metal box on the wall.

'Dratted thing,' muttered Bard, giving up and chucking the receipt in the bin. 'Oh yes, there's something I been meaning to ask you. Has that father of yours got back to you yet?'

'What?'

'About you stopping here?'

Kit was still looking at the box on the wall. 'Is that some kind of a safe?' she asked pointing at it. 'What do you keep in it?'

'Keys. Don't change the subject. Have you heard from him or not?'

'Yeah,' said Kit vaguely.

'And he's OK with you being here is he?'

'Fine, really happy.' She was still focused on the metal box and wasn't really thinking about what she was saying. If that was the Moonstone key safe, then it probably contained keys to every room in the museum, including Captain John's portrait gallery.

'Happy?' Bard was surprised. 'And he's definitely told your brother and sister where you are?'

'What? Oh, er, yes,' said Kit.

'Well that's a weight off my mind at any rate,' said Bard, and Kit instantly felt guilty. She began backing out of the room before he could ask any more awkward questions.

'By the way,' he called after her. 'You been messing with some of the walking sticks in the rabology room? Every time I go in there, looks as if someone's been mucking around with them.'

Kit pretended not to hear and hurried back up to her room. She didn't like being dishonest. She hadn't planned on lying to her grandfather like that. It felt mean and wrong, but what else could she have done? Anyway, telling the old man a few white lies was nothing compared to the crime she was now considering committing— sneaking into his office, to steal a key that didn't belong to her. She felt sick at the thought.

* * *

Finding an opportunity to carry out the theft turned out to be trickier than she expected. The old man seemed to be taking his bookkeeping very seriously and sat stubbornly at his desk for most of the day. All Kit could do was loiter around the flat, hoping that she would get a chance at some point.

It came at last in the afternoon, when a violently loud jangling sound brought her running down from the attic.

'Is it the fire alarm,' she asked breathlessly.

'Don't talk daft,' said Bard, standing precariously on a chair to switch the buzzer off. 'Fire alarm hasn't worked for about ten years. It's the public doorbell. Means the museum's got a visitor.'

'Oh,' said Kit. 'I never noticed a bell before.'

'You'd better stop up here out of the way while I go down to attend to them.'

Kit didn't argue. This was her chance to look for the key. She waited a moment to make sure Bard had really gone, then tiptoed into his office, heading straight for the metal box on the wall. Reaching up, she pulled on the little handle, but it wouldn't open—locked, of course.

So now she had another key to find, before she could find the key that she was actually looking for. Her eyes scoured the room. Where would Bard keep such a thing? There were no drawers in the desk and the only other possibility was the filing cabinet. She knelt down in front of it. The metal door made a thunderous noise as she pulled it wide. Kit began flipping through the folders as fast as she could.

Most of them contained information about objects in the Moonstone collection, clocks, musical instruments, and costumes. Right at the back, she came across one marked Children's Clothes. She hesitated. In spite of the need for haste. Kit couldn't help having a look. She pulled the folder open and felt inside.

There was hardly anything in there, just a single sheet of thick, yellowed paper, an ancient record of some sort. It took her a moment to decipher the old-fashioned handwriting.

Item 1.
Description: Young child's bodice and skirt, made of brocaded Spitalfields silk.
Date: Mid-18th Century
Place of Origin: England

Historical Note: Worn by Minna

Silk-Hatton of Moonstone Manor during the celebration of her third birthday.

Item 2.
Description: Girl's gown and petticoat, made of mushroom-colored silk, with woven floral pattern.
Date: Mid-18th Century
Place of Origin: England
Historical Note: Worn by Fenella Silk-Hatton, of Moonstone Manor, during the celebration of her sister Minna's third birthday.

General Comment.
Despite the ten-year age gap of these two sisters, they were known to have been inseparable. This may have been in part due to the premature loss of their mother and the fact that Fenella Silk-Hatton suffered from a severe form of selective mutism. The fact that both garments have survived serves as a touching tribute to the girls' devotion to each other.

For a moment, Kit was bewildered by the shock. Then her eyes filled with tears and the memory of Fenella's frantic searching last night came back to her. Minna was her little sister. A child of only three, lost and alone. No wonder Fenella was so distraught. With their mother dead, she must have been like a parent to Minna, just as Albert and Roz were to her. This similarity made her wonder what her own siblings would do if she went missing. Somehow she couldn't imagine them being as desperate to find her as Fenella was to find Minna.

She pushed the thought aside and returned to the document, tracing her finger under the words 'selective mutism'. Kit had never met anyone who suffered from this condition, but she knew what it was, an anxiety disorder that meant you found it impossible to speak in most social situations. So this explained why Fenella never talked. Kit didn't think she would ever forget the agony of those silent sobs.

But there was something more in the document. She didn't see it at first, but soon it began to dawn on her. If Kit's grandmother, Katherine, was a relative of the Silk-Hattons who had lived in Moonstone, and Fenella and Minna were also from that family, then Kit herself must be related to them too. She imagined the Silk-Hatton line stretching down the ages from Fenella, all the way to her. It was an electrifying thought.

Kit was brought back to her surroundings by a noise. Was that Bard returning? In a panic, she jammed the paper back in the folder, closed the filing cabinet and leapt to her feet. She tugged frantically at the door to the key safe again and then in desperation, felt on top of it, just in case Bard had put the key there. Her fingers closed around a hard object – unbelievable! She almost laughed out loud. How typical of Bard to go to all the bother of locking up a safe and then hide the key on top of it.

In a flash she had the door open and was examining the keys inside. Each one was labelled. Kit fumbled through them—oriental room, long walk, nursery, rabology room, portrait gallery—here it was. She unhooked it quickly, locked the safe door, and in less than a minute was strolling casually out of the flat with the key in her pocket.

* * *

There was no sign of Bard after all. The old man was obviously still in the museum somewhere, showing the visitors around. As long as he was nowhere near the west wing she could slip along there now and try the key out.

Kit walked quickly, stopping every now and then to listen. When she reached the hall balcony she was relieved to hear voices downstairs and sped silently towards the rabology room. Soon the door to the portrait gallery was in front of her and, with trembling fingers, she fitted the key into the lock. It turned easily and in a moment she had whisked the door open, slipped inside, and locked it behind her.

An acrid, bitter smell met her and Kit instantly knew why Bard had refused to let her see this room. There had been a fire. One corner of it was badly burned, the wood panelling charred black. It was a terrible sight, by far the worst thing Kit had seen at Moonstone, and she realized how close the place must have come to burning down. She couldn't bear to think what would have happened to Bard and all the costumes if that had happened.

The gallery was almost empty except for a large wooden plinth. There was also a colossal painting on the wall which was so thickly covered in soot that she couldn't see the picture at all. It was a horrible looking thing, like a framed black hole. Why was Captain John so keen to gain entry to this room?

Then Kit noticed something else. In the corner, where the fire must have started, was another door. Of course, this must be the entrance to the second gallery, the one that had been labelled 'the summer room' on her mum's map. As she approached an idea occurred to her. Could Minna be in there? Surely this was the obvious explanation. It was the only room in the museum that had not yet been searched. The little girl must be shut inside. As this realization dawned on her, Kit's nightmare suddenly rushed back into her mind—the sensation of being trapped, the smell of burning . . . this is what had happened to Minna.

With a buzz of excitement, Kit grasped the burnt looking door handle and pressed down, but there was no response. She pressed again. Was this door locked as well? She would have to go back and get the key. She rattled the handle one more time and then something awful happened. It came away in her hand. She stared at it in horror. What had she done? She tried to put it back, but it was hopeless. On closer inspection she realized that the brass doorplate was completely melted, the lock distorted and twisted. No key or handle would ever open that door again.

CHAPTER 10

Kit was distraught. Had she just ruined Fenella's last hope of finding Minna? There was no other way into the summer room. How could the sisters ever be reunited now? She pictured a lonely little figure toddling up and down a room with flowery wallpaper. She was only three years old. She wouldn't understand why Fenella never came for her.

Kit couldn't bear to stay there any longer. She laid the broken handle on the floor and fled across the room to the other entrance. She wrenched the door open and turned back to lock it.

'Afternoon,' said a voice behind her.

Kit yelped, dropped the key on the floor and

spun round. Finn Scudder was sitting on a spindle-legged chair, with his legs propped up on one of the display buckets, smiling.

'You look like you've just been caught stealing the crown jewels,' he said.

Kit cleared cleared her throat. 'Are you . . . are you looking for my grandfather?'

'No,' his eyes rested significantly on the key at her feet. 'I think I've found what I was looking for.'

Kit swallowed and pretended not to understand. 'He's showing a visitor around the museum.'

'Oh I know who he's with. Bloke by the name of Graham Groid. I brought him along. He's the Senior Arts Operation Manager for the local authority.'

'You mean he's from the council?'

'That's it. He's quite a bigwig actually. Has a lot of influence. Thought it would be good for him to experience Moonstone at first hand. It's hard to do it justice with pictures.' He sniffed exaggeratedly. 'Have you noticed a funny smell round here, like an old bonfire or something?'

Kit shook her head quickly and tried not to let the panic register in her face.

'You'd better pick that key up. Gramps won't be happy if you lose it will he?'

She did as she was told, bending quickly. The key felt heavy in her hand and she wished that it was still safely in Bard's office and that she'd never taken it out.

'Look at the state of your hands. What have you been doing to get yourself in such a mess?'

'Nothing,' said Kit, putting them quickly behind her back.

'Is that right. Amazing how dirty you can get when you're doing nothing. Tell me, where does that door lead?'

'Nowhere,' said Kit, then remembering Bard's original lie she said; 'It's a cleaning cupboard. I've been cleaning you know, polishing stuff, that's why my hands are black.'

Finn lifted his feet off the display bucket and stood up. He was a thin weasel of a man, but he was still a lot bigger than Kit.

'See, it's a funny thing,' he said, 'but when I had a look round last time I was here, I was sure there was something different about the museum, you know, something missing. So I did a bit of digging around in our local archives and you'll never guess what I found.' He flipped open the folder he was carrying and pulled out a sheet of paper. 'An old plan of this house from when it was first built, back in the eighteenth century. I took a copy. You can have a look if you like.'

He placed it on the chair seat. 'So that's how I know for a fact that there are two more rooms on the other side of that door, and what I want to know is, why they've been locked up? Must be something pretty bad for your granddad to actually close a gallery, he doesn't have any shame about the mess in the rest of the place.'

'It's just a cleaning cupboard,' insisted Kit.

'Do you know what I think?' said Finn with a sneer. 'I think Granddad has had a bit of a fire in there and that's why he's locked the door. Trying to cover it up so no one knows what a lousy job he's been doing of looking after Moonstone. Imagine what Graham Groid is going to say when he finds out he nearly burnt the place down.'

'It's not true,' said Kit, pressing her back against the door. If only she'd managed to lock it, she could have made a run for it. But if she tried that now, there would be nothing stopping Finn Scudder.

The property developer seemed to read what was in her mind and laughed. He took a step towards her but at that very moment there was a loud crash somewhere in the museum, followed by a bellow of rage.

'What the hell?' said Finn, swinging round. He listened and then hurried out of the gallery in the direction of the disturbance.

Kit remained where she was for a moment. What on earth was going on? Had Bard been hurt? She raced after Finn, leaving the door of the portrait gallery unlocked behind her.

* * *

It wasn't difficult to find the source of the commotion. As Kit ran down the stairs, she could hear the sound of raised voices coming from the library. By the time she reached the hall Finn was already inside, and she hurtled after him, dashed through the door and nearly fell over something on the floor.

'Idiot child,' said an angry voice.

Kit regained her balance and stared. The thing she had nearly tripped over, turned out to be a man. He was sitting on the floor, red with rage, and all around him, scattered like matches, were walking sticks from the rabology room.

'What do you think you are doing, careering around in a museum like that? Could have done me a serious injury.'

'Sorry,' said Kit.

'What's been going on here, Graham?' said Finn, helping the man to his feet.

'A good question,' he said. 'Mr Trench here

obviously thought it would be a funny joke
to ambush me with a pile of walking sticks
balanced on top of a door.'

'What?'

'I never had nothing to do with it,' said Bard,
peering at the door in a mystified way. 'No idea
how all those sticks got up there.'

Bard might have been in the dark but Kit was
fairly sure she knew who was responsible.

'Well, if it wasn't you, then I'd like to know
who did do it,' snapped Graham Groid, now
back on his feet.

Bard shrugged helplessly.

'It was . . . it was me,' said Kit, and three sets
of eyes swivelled in her direction.

'Who is this girl?'

'Er, she's my granddaughter. She's stopping
at Moonstone just now, but she won't be here
much longer,' said Bard, directing a poisonous
look at Kit. 'You'd better clear up all these sticks
while I finish giving Mr Groid his tour.'

'Thank you, but I've seen quite enough
already,' said the man, and began irritably
brushing the dust off his trousers. 'I
accompanied Finn Scudder to this place with
an open mind. I was hoping there might have
been some mistake and we could avoid carrying
out a full enquiry, but I see I was wrong. This

museum is a disgrace.'

'I did warn you, Graham,' said Finn. He was so smug and self-satisfied in his flashy black suit that Kit wanted to hit him. By comparison, Bard looked old and shabby and there was something vulnerable about the way he was standing there that made Kit's heart ache.

'P'raps if you come up and have a look in the other galleries . . .' Bard began.

'Oh, yeah,' said Finn with relish. 'It's even better upstairs. There's a couple of rooms in the west wing that I think you'll find particularly interesting.'

But Graham Groid held up a hand. 'Thank you Finn, but Mr Trench will have ample opportunity to show me everything when I return in three weeks' time, accompanied by the inspector.' He glanced down at his diary. 'I think Friday the 28th of August is free.'

'Inspector?' repeated Bard blankly. 'What Inspector?'

'The Regional Inspector for Culture and Arts. It will be up to him to decide whether to close this museum or not, but from what I've seen here today, I have no doubt that the site will be sold immediately to Mr Scudder.'

And with these words, he gave his trousers one last angry brush and marched out of the building. Finn followed behind. At the door he paused to wink at Kit.

'Thanks kid, I owe you one. See you on the 28th.'

* * *

For a long time after they had gone Bard didn't speak. Neither did Kit, she was staring at the floor.

'Well, that's that then,' grunted Bard finally and slumped down onto an old chair with the stuffing coming out. All the fight seemed to have gone out of him.

'I'm so s—'

'Don't apologize,' said Bard. 'Too late for that, though what you were thinking of, putting those sticks up on top of the door, I don't know.'

Kit pressed her lips together. It was awful not being able to tell him the truth.

The old man sat glumly for a while and then rubbed his head with his hands. 'But I shouldn't blame you. Probably wouldn't have made no difference. Even if you hadn't dumped half a ton of walking sticks on the man's head, he'd still have made the same decision once he'd seen the rest of the place.'

Kit was surprised by this forbearance, but

there was a question eating away at her that she had to ask.

'What will happen to the costumes if . . . ?'

'If Moonstone is sold?' said Bard, finishing the sentence for her. He sighed. 'If they were in better nick, they'd be auctioned off, but I don't think there's much chance of that.' He shook his head. 'Council won't want the bother of trying to get rid of them if there's no money to be made. They'll probably just make a big bonfire and burn the lot.'

'Burn them,' said Kit. She felt dizzy with shock. Never for a moment had she thought this was a possibility. She pictured Fenella being dragged out into the grounds, then hurled on top of a great pyre of burning costumes.

Kit sat down weakly on another chair. 'We've still got three weeks,' she whispered.

'Three weeks,' he scoffed. 'What do you think I can achieve in that time? Just about manage to sweep the floor and put a couple of pictures straight. Three weeks indeed.'

'I'll help. My dad doesn't come back until the 27th, I can stay until then.'

Bard actually laughed. 'Well that'll make all the difference, that will.'

'But we can't do nothing. We've got to try and save Moonstone.'

He raised a wintery face and shook his head. 'I should have listened to your dad, shouldn't I?' he said bitterly. 'He told me I was mad to stay here on my own and he was right. See what I've brought the place to—a conference centre for Finn Scudder. What would your mum say if she knew?'

'It's not too late,' persisted Kit.

'Yes it is. It was too late the day your mum left, I just didn't want to admit it. We got to face it, Moonstone is as good as lost.'

Bard rose painfully from the chair and shuffled out of the room. Kit watched him go, and it was all she could do to fight back the tears.

* * *

Kit walked numbly through the galleries looking for Fenella and found her at last, standing on her plinth in the nursery. She gazed at her pale face and the beautiful mushroom-coloured gown and hated Finn Scudder with a violence that she had never experienced before.

Feeling lost and desperate, she climbed the spiral staircase to the sewing room in the attic. The sunshine poured through the windows. Ironically, it was the first nice day since she had arrived at Moonstone.

She pulled out a stool from under the table and sat down bleakly, paddling her finger in the dust. Then she picked up the tweezers, so like the ones in her own sewing box, and started to think about her mum. What would she have done in this situation? Would she have given up and allowed Moonstone be sold and the costumes destroyed? Would she have let a man like Finn Scudder win? Or would she have done something to try and stop him?

In her pocket was the old museum pamphlet she had brought with her from home. She took it out and studied the picture. Even though it was faded and creased, she could see how different the house looked. The grounds were neat and tidy, the windows looked clean and well painted. This was a different Moonstone, a Moonstone in its prime, when Katherine and Emmie had lived here with Bard and the place had been loved and cared for. But it hadn't always been like that. When her grandparents had first arrived, the museum had been in a terrible condition and they had rescued it from being sold by restoring it to its former glory.

Now Moonstone was facing a worse threat, and surely the only way to save it was to do something similar—clean the place up, mend the costumes, hack back the overgrown gardens. But how could she do this on her own? She was only twelve years old, what did she know about renovating a historic house? And there were only three weeks before the inspection day. It was impossible.

And then, just when she was ready to give up, the solution came to her—the costumes of course, all the ladies and gents in their historic dress, they could help. There were loads of them, an army of assistants ready and waiting. They would surely jump at the chance to save their home—especially if their very existence depended on it. All she had to do was ask.

CHAPTER 11

It was one thing to have a brilliant idea, it was another to put it into action, and as the afternoon and evening dragged by, Kit got increasingly nervous about how she was going to broach the subject with the night-time inhabitants of Moonstone. The thought of trying to make some kind of speech filled her with terror. What if they didn't take her seriously, what if they laughed? Her stomach knotted up with anxiety and she felt the way she did before a confrontation with her dad. He never listened to her, so why would a large crowd of mannequins in historic costume?

At last the sun set behind the distant hills, but it was still too early to go out into the museum. Kit switched on the lamp and stood at her bedroom window, watching the pale moths flutter through the tall grass down below. Slowly the stars emerged in the sky like tiny sequins stitched to a great cloth. Kit pulled a chair up to the window and leaned on the sill, resting her tired head in her arms. Then she closed her eyes.

The next thing she knew it was dark outside. Her cheek seemed to be stuck to her bare arm and her neck had a one-sided crick in it. She peeled her face off her arm and tried to rotate her head round in the opposite direction.

'Ahh!'

Fenella was standing right next to her, they were almost nose to nose. She was clasping her hands tightly together and looked frightened and upset.

'What's the matter?' asked Kit immediately.

Fenella didn't answer, but she moved quickly to the door and beckoned urgently. Kit hurried after her, wondering uneasily what had gone wrong in the museum now. She assumed that they were heading for the great hall, but it was empty, except for Giles Clanker, who was stumping along, as usual, on some unknown mission of his own. Fenella skirted around the balcony and led the way into the cogs.

'Where are we going?' said Kit. Fenella stopped suddenly and put her finger to her lips, listening intently.

Kit listened too and at that moment, she heard it for the first time; the long drawn out wail of someone in terrible pain. The sound of it froze her blood.

Together they crept onwards. Every now and then, another cry echoed through the galleries and they would clasp hands tightly and wait until it had passed. When, at length, they reached the rabology room Kit got another surprise. The door to the portrait gallery was standing wide open, and she remembered that in all the excitement she had completely forgotten to go back and lock it. The key was still in her pocket.

Through the opening, a strange sight met her eyes. Every museum mannequin in historic dress appeared to be crammed into the fire-damaged room. They had their backs to the door and their eyes were fixed on the wooden plinth. Captain John was pacing there, like a wild animal, lashing his sleeves in a frenzy, between howls of misery. At his feet was a pile of walking sticks and he suddenly ran at them, kicking them furiously into the crowd.

'This is intolerable,' cried Kiko Kai, who had,

unfortunately, been whacked on the head by one of the flying sticks. 'Is there nothing you can do to make the man stop?'

'Certainly there is,' said a harassed looking Lady Ann, surreptitiously trying to untangle a second stick from her back drapes. 'But he must be allowed to grieve. He has sustained a terrible shock. Have a little compassion, for pity's sake?'

'It is hard to feel compassion for someone who has just hit me with a walking cane. We are not accustomed to such excessive displays of emotion in the nineteenth century. We must have more self-control than you.'

'Self-control? Poppycock! Why, Claudia Clack never stops weeping from one day to the next,' said Lady Ann, pointing to the lady in the black mourning gown, who was yet again dabbing her cheeks with a handkerchief.

'A little decorous weeping is appropriate for a lady in her situation, but there is nothing decorous,' said Kiko, her voice rising to make herself heard over another bellow from the Captain, 'ABOUT THAT HULLABALOO!'

Lady Ann seemed at a loss what to do next. 'For heaven's sake do something,' she hissed at Sir Jasper Stockings, who was standing next to her. 'You're a man. You must know how to cheer him up.'

'Oh, ahh,' said Sir Jasper, looking extremely uncomfortable. 'Not really my area of expertise.' He sidled forward and reached up to pat Captain John awkwardly on one arm. 'There, there, old fellow. Never mind about your portrait. I'm sure you'll get used to the loss soon enough.'

But this seemed to make the captain worse. He raised both his arms in the air, looked at the blackened painting on the wall opposite and let out a piercing shriek. Sir Jasper shot away from him in alarm.

Back in the doorway, an inkling of the truth had just begun to dawn on Kit. She nudged Fenella and pointed at the picture on the wall.

'Was that a portrait of Captain John?' she whispered. 'Does he think that it's been destroyed by the fire?'

Fenella nodded sadly.

Kit started frantically searching her pockets. She found an old tissue in one and then hunted round for something to stand on. Her eyes fastened on one of the walking-stick buckets and she emptied it quickly. Then, carrying it with her, she crept silently behind the crowd of costumes and positioned it upside down, directly under the portrait. Testing it for strength, she stood up on it cautiously.

Her face was now very close to the glazed

surface and she could see how the costumes might have been fooled. The picture was completely hidden behind a solid layer of velvety black, and for a moment she wondered if she was wrong. Well, there was only one way to find out. She chose a central spot in the upper part of the painting and began to rub the glass carefully with the tissue. The soot had a stubborn, stuck-on quality, but Kit kept at it and soon she had cleaned a tiny window. Through it, a man's painted eye stared out at her and, just for a second, she imagined that it winked.

By now, Fenella had joined her by the painting. She was hopping up and down with excitement, her normally pale face flushed. Kit went on wiping, until she had enlarged the window to reveal the whole of the man's face and the upper part of his body. It was enough for her to be certain that the picture was an exact portrait of Captain John, right down to the embroidered, floral motifs that decorated his muslin robe. Kit didn't know much about museum objects, but she guessed how rare this combination of portrait and costume must be. The two unmistakably belonged together and she could understand why their separation had traumatized the captain so much.

Fenella could no longer contain herself. She

wasn't able to speak, but she pushed her way through the crowd until she reached Captain John, then bravely tugged the end of one of his long sleeves and pointed towards the picture. For a moment he looked furious, then confused and finally he gasped and stood, transfixed.

'My face,' he whispered. 'My dear old face. Look, it's come back. How is it possible?'

Other costumes were turning to look now and Kit could hear their murmured exclamations. For the second time in two days, she found herself the focus of their collective attention and she turned around awkwardly on her makeshift plinth and tried to smile.

'It's just soot,' she explained. 'You know, from the fire. It needs cleaning off, that's all.'

Across the room, she could see the captain, his face now euphoric. He seized a terrified looking Claudia Clack, hauled her up beside him and began waltzing her around in circles.

Sir Jasper Stockings beamed across the room at her. 'Bravo, young sir,' he said. 'Do you suppose you'll be able to uncover all of the portrait?'

'I think so, I just need some better cleaning equipment.' Kit held up the scrap of tissue which was now black with grime. 'This is hopeless. I'll have to find a microfiber cloth and some glass-cleaning spray.'

'Will you, by Jove,' said Sir Jasper enthusiastically, although he clearly had no idea what she was talking about.

'One moment, Sir Jasper,' said a haughty voice and Kit saw to her alarm that Lady Ann Hoops was now scything her way through the crowd towards her. 'I would like to express my gratitude to this child for her assistance.' Lady Ann stretched out her hand.

'Oh, er, thanks,' said Kit, taken aback by this unexpected honour. She wasn't sure what she was supposed to do and glanced uncertainly at Fenella, who mimed a curtsy. Kit had never done such a thing in her life and certainly not while standing on a bucket being gawped at by a mob of museum mannequins in historic costumes. Acutely embarrassed, she bent her knees awkwardly and ended up doing a sort of bow.

Lady Ann let go of her hand hastily. 'Of course, if there is anything we can do for you in return, you have only to say,' she added coldly.

Kit hesitated. It was too good to be true, wasn't it? An actual invitation from Lady Ann to make a request. Her heart started to beat rapidly. This was it. There would never be a better opportunity to ask the costumes for their help.

'Ac . . . actually, there was something I wanted to ask,' stuttered Kit. She stopped and looked out over the sea of faces. There were an awful lot of them and they were all waiting expectantly for her to say something. She cleared her throat several times.

Sir Jasper nodded at her encouragingly.

'The thing is,' said Kit at last. 'I found out some bad news today about Moonstone. It's in such a mess that the current owners want to sell it and turn it into a conference centre.'

'What on earth is a conference centre?' asked Kiko, sliding out of the crowd and joining Lady Ann by the portrait.

'It's a . . . it's a . . . Well, it doesn't really matter what it is,' said Kit, feeling the impossibility of explaining such a thing to someone from the nineteenth century. 'The point is that Moonstone won't be a museum any more, and that means you will lose your home.'

There was an eruption among the costumes—'Moonstone not a museum any more?' 'Lose our home?' 'What is the child talking about?'

But Kit was only too aware that this wasn't the worst of it. She knew that she ought to tell them about the real danger in which they stood, but she shied away from the task. How could she articulate something so dreadful—oh by the way, it's likely that you'll all be thrown away, or worse—Kit couldn't bring herself to say it.

'Wait a minute,' she said, flapping her arms to try and restore calm. 'I've got an idea about what we can do to keep Moonstone safe, but it's going to mean a lot of hard work and there's only three weeks to do it in.'

'To do what in?' said Lady Ann, frowning crossly. Clearly, she hadn't expected Kit to take up her offer.

'Restore the museum,' said Kit. 'You know, tidy it up, mend the things that are broken, give the place a good clean.'

A look of horrified incredulity was spreading over Lady Ann's face. 'Are you suggesting that I, Lady Ann Hoops, should debase myself with domestic chores?'

'Er, y . . . yes.'

'But that's servants' work!'

'Oh,' said Kit. She hadn't considered that the costumes might look at it in this way.

'Perhaps, you should ask Kiko Kai,' said Lady Ann in an affronted tone. 'They might be more accustomed to that kind of thing in the nineteenth century.'

'We most certainly are not,' said Kiko rising to the challenge immediately. 'None of us would

148

ever consider disgracing ourselves by assisting with such work.' Her eyes travelled around the room, defying anyone to contradict her.

'I promise you, there's nothing disgraceful about cleaning,' said Kit, but it was too late. The damage was done. Kiko had turned her back and was already gliding towards the door and Lady Ann, with her short, staccato strides, wasn't far behind.

'Don't dawdle,' she barked and, one after another, everyone shuffled out of the room. Some of them paused and looked back, as if they would have liked to ask more, but they were no match for Kiko Kai and Lady Ann Hoops, and soon Kit and Fenella were completely alone.

Kit climbed down from the bucket feeling defeated. As she'd expected, no one had listened to her. She had failed completely. She kicked herself for not disclosing all the facts. How could she expect them to understand the seriousness of the situation when she hadn't told them?

Fenella was standing close by, a look of concern on her face, as if it was she who was worrying about Kit, instead of the other way around. She had her back to the burned door and Kit could see the broken handle on the floor. Another wave of guilt swept over her. Fenella didn't know the half of it.

'Fenella,' said Kit in a small voice. 'There's something I've got to tell you.' She hesitated and then led her over to the charred door and told her everything. She described her recurring nightmare about the summer room, her suspicions that Minna was inside it and how the handle had broken off when she tried to use it.

Fenella was at the door immediately, pushing on it, hitting it frantically. She picked up the twisted piece of metal and tried to fit it back into place, just as Kit had done. But it was useless. At last she turned back to Kit and the helpless despair in her face was terrible to see.

'Listen, Fenella,' said Kit. 'We'll get Minna out of there, I promise. I just need some time to work out how. What we've got to focus on now, is finding a way to save Moonstone, or the museum will be sold before we can rescue her.'

Fenella's head was bowed. 'Do you understand what I'm saying?' asked Kit. The little head nodded.

After that, the two girls slowly retraced their steps until they were back in Bard's flat. Fenella made no move to leave and Kit sat cross-legged on her pillow feeling wretched as the girl wandered blindly around her bedroom, randomly picking up objects and putting them down again.

It was when she touched her mum's old sewing box that there was a change. It was as if Fenella came suddenly awake. She placed the box down on the table and opened it with an eagerness that surprised Kit. Her face lit up with something like recognition. She put out her hand to touch the things inside, lifting the scissors carefully to inspect them, popping the thimble on her finger.

There was something in the way that she handled the tools that made Kit uncross her legs and sit up.

'Fenella,' she said. 'Can you sew?'

Fenella nodded vigorously. She lifted the hem of her gown with one hand, twirled in a circle and curtsied.

'You made your own dress?' said Kit, starting to feel excited. She gazed at the beautiful gown the girl was wearing. 'That is seriously impressive. Maybe you could teach me.'

Suddenly Kit was on her feet, dancing Fenella round in circles. 'Why didn't you tell me this before, you idiot? This might change everything. If you can sew then maybe there still is something we can do to save the museum.'

CHAPTER 12

Kit soon had a plan sketched out in her head.
She may not have been very good at passing
school exams, but she was still the daughter
of Sir Henry Halliwell and her brain worked
quickly. She could do nothing, however, without
Fenella's agreement, and she spent some time
explaining her idea.'

Once Fenella understood, she was all in
favour and keen to get started. Kit sent her off to
search for Winifred Ware, the lady in the bustle
that Finn Scudder had damaged.

Once Fenella had departed, Kit crept back
down the attic stairs and, with some difficulty,
extracted Bard's Hoover from a cupboard.
She paused to listen, but could still hear the

reassuring sound of the old man's snores coming from his bedroom. He really did sleep as deeply as he claimed.

The Hoover was old-fashioned and heavy, and it was hard work lugging it up the spiral stairs to the sewing room. She switched the lights on and looked around.

By the time Fenella arrived, she had already cleaned the table and had just finished vacuuming the floor. The studio was looking a lot better, although she wished she'd had time to dust the large storage chest that held all the sewing equipment.

'Bless my soul,' gasped Winifred Ware, tottering up the last few steps into the sewing room, helped by Fenella. There was horrible tearing sound. 'Oh do be careful, Edith dear, that's the fourth time you've trodden on my damaged train.'

These words were directed at a third figure who was coming up behind them. It turned out to be Winifred's companion from the library, the woman that was so thickly covered in dust that Kit had drawn a line through it with her finger. She could see the brown slash of colour on her gown now, and imagined how much better it would look if it could be cleaned.

The new arrival didn't pay any attention to

Winifred's words and stomped nosily up the
steps into the studio, crashing straight into
a chair. She squinted short-sightedly at Kit
through a pair of cloudy spectacles and held out
her hand.

'I'm Edith Butcher,' she said gruffly. 'But I
prefer to be called Nurse.'

'Oh,' said Kit. 'I thought you were a maid.'

'Do I look like one? I've never heard of a maid
who had human blood stains down the front of
their gown. Mind you,' she added sadly. 'I'm so
dusty these days that no one can actually see 'um
any more.'

'Er . . . that's a shame,' said Kit. She was
distracted by Winifred who, having looked
warily around the room, was now edging back
towards the exit.

'Please don't go,' said Kit, heading her off.
'We want to help you.' But when Winifred
learned what Kit had in mind she was aghast.

'Oh no,' she said faintly. 'I could never give
my consent to such a scheme, never. Allow a
child from the eighteenth century to stich up my
poor torn frills? What would Kiko Kai say?'

'She won't know anything about it,' said Kit.
'And Fenella is very experienced at sewing.'

'Don't know what you're making such a fuss
about, Winny,' said the nurse, tripping over

155

the Hoover. 'If you don't do something about it soon, that lace of yours is going to part company with you for good. I'd snap at the chance if someone offered to clean me up.'

Kit considered these words for a moment. A crazy idea had just popped into her head and she didn't know if she dared mention it or not.

'Have you ever heard of a Hoover or a vacuum cleaner?' she asked the nurse cautiously. 'It's a sort of modern machine that sucks up dust.'

Nurse Butcher looked interested. 'A clothes-dusting machine? Clever.'

'Well actually,' admitted Kit, 'they're normally used on the floor, but I don't see why we couldn't try it on you.'

Winifred, in the meantime, had approached the table.

'Oh dear me, look at all those pins and needles,' she said shuddering in a way that reminded Kit of how she felt when she visited the dentist.

'You think they look bad,' said the nurse unhelpfully. 'We used to cut people's legs off with a rusty saw.'

Fenella quickly intervened by turning Winnifred gently away from the table and looking at her beseechingly.

'Please let us help,' begged Kit.

Winifred hesitated, looking from one to the other.

'Tell you what,' said the nurse, making up for her previous remark about the rusty saw. 'If you allow Fenella to stitch back your frills, I'll let this other one have a crack at cleaning me up with her facuum-prover.'

Winifred was persuaded at last.

There was some doubt as to where they should seat her while the work was in progress. Realizing that it would be difficult for Fenella to kneel on the floor for long periods of time, Kit suggested they get her to climb on to the table. This was a difficult operation, requiring the combined efforts of Kit, Fenella and Nurse Butcher, but it was accomplished in the end.

Kit positioned a chair for Winifred and then then hesitated.

'Can she actually sit down with all that stuff at the back?' she whispered to the nurse, looking doubtfully at Winifred's voluminous backside.

'Certainly I can,' said Winifred, overhearing. 'My bustle frame simply collapses.'

'Silly fashion if you ask me,' muttered the nurse, accidently knocking a pair of scissors onto the floor. 'You wouldn't catch a working girl like me wearing anything under her gown except some decent, heavy-duty petticoats.'

Winifred seemed keen to demonstrate to them the best method for sitting down when wearing a bustle.

'If you wouldn't mind holding the chair for me dear,' she asked Kit. 'They do have a nasty habit of traveling backwards if there is no one to restrain them.'

Kit grasped the wooden legs and tried not to catch Fenella's eye in case she got the giggles.

'The first step is to sweep your train to the side,' she said, passing one arm behind her bustle and scooping her skirts to the right. 'Then you approach your seat cautiously in reverse and lower yourself slowly, until you are seated, thus.'

Winifred was now perched, rigidly upright, on the extreme edge of her chair.

'Right,' said Kit. 'Are you sure you're comfortable like that?'

'Of course she's not comfortable,' said the nurse scornfully. 'How can she be when she's wearing a chemise, a pair of drawers, a corset, a bustle frame and two petticoats, not to mention an extremely heavy satin bodice and skirt with an extensive train?'

Kit was staggered by this list of clothing. Was it normal to wear so many layers in the nineteenth century? She wondered what Lady Ann Hoops wore under her gown to make it stick out as it did, but she doubted she would ever find the courage to ask.

Kit had already assembled what Fenella would need. As well as the pins and needles, there were several thimbles of different sizes, a tape measure, tweezers, scissors, and a variety of different threads. With delicate fingers, Fenella began by inspecting Winifred's torn lace. Using the tweezers, she removed the loose threads and pinned it carefully back in place. Then she selected a fine needle and some matching cream thread and started to sew.

Kit now turned her attention to the nurse. Despite her no-nonsense attitude, Nurse Butcher looked a little apprehensive as Kit pulled the vacuum cleaner towards her and plugged it in. She pulled off the wide suction head, held up the hose and was just about to switch the machine on when she suddenly panicked. If this went wrong, she could potentially damage the costume quite badly. The Hoover might be old, but it was powerful and the moment she put it anywhere near the dusty gown it would surely suck as much of the fabric down the pipe as could fit.

'Is there a problem?' said the nurse impatiently. 'Why aren't you getting on with it?'

'I've just thought of something I need,' said

Kit and dashed over to the chest of tools. She pulled out several drawers and at last found one that contained paint brushes.

'Perfect,' murmured Kit feeling the soft bristles with her hand. It was almost as if the brushes were there for this very reason.

She switched on the Hoover and cautiously tried out her newly invented technique. Rather than applying the suction directly to the fabric, she held it a short distance away and used the paintbrush to gently stroke the dust from the surface of the gown into the hose. It wasn't fast, but it was much safer and still very effective. Slowly, Nurse Butcher's dress turned from lumpy grey to brown.

Once she had got used to it, the nurse seemed to enjoy herself. The sensation of being vacuumed turned out to be quite pleasant, and Kit completed the treatment by cleaning her glasses, so she could see properly again.

Meanwhile, Fenella worked steadily around the hem of Winifred's gown, reattaching her torn lace and flounces. After that she mended an ugly rip in her pleated side panel and secured three buttons down the front of her bodice. When everything was done, she was passed her over to Kit for a vacuum, while Fenella patched some holes in the nurse's bodice.

By the time they had finished the two costumes were transformed. Winifred Ware and Nurse Butcher couldn't stop admiring themselves in the mirror and kept jostling each other out of the way so they could get a better view.

'What will everyone say when they see me?' said Winifred exultantly. 'I can't wait to show myself off to Sita Chakrabarti. She'll turn green with envy.'

'And look at my bloodstains' said the nurse with ghoulish delight. 'You can see them as clearly now as the day they were made.'

This reaction was exactly what Kit had been hoping for and, once she had managed to drag them away from the mirror, she hurried the two women down the spiral stairs. As the sound of their footsteps faded, Kit and Fenella looked at each questioningly. It was too soon to know if the plan was going to work yet, but they had given it their best shot. Now there was nothing to do but wait and see how quickly the word spread.

* * *

To keep Fenella's mind off Minna and stop Kit from falling asleep, they decided to have a sewing lesson. Kit was used to receiving one-to-one tuition, but this was completely different because Fenella couldn't talk. She made a wonderful teacher, though, kind and encouraging and never impatient. First she showed Kit how to thread a needle and then she gave her a scrap of calico and made her practise different kinds of stiches.

They were so absorbed in what they were doing that when there came a sudden clatter of footsteps from below, they were completely unprepared. Kit pricked her finger on her needle and Fenella dropped a reel of cotton. Nervously, Kit got to her feet.

Up the stairs came not one person, but five, the man in the Chinese dragon robe, the ballet dancer, both the gentlemen wearing dressing gowns and the Inuit. They were all talking at the same time and came surging into the room towards her.

'My lining is in tatters.'

'My wings are falling off.'

'Can you sew up my side seams?'

'I'm all over splits.'

'Help me, help me, I think there's something eating my fur?'

For a moment, Kit felt overwhelmed, but then she felt something brush against her and

Fenella was by her side. Her calm presence was reassuring and Kit took a deep breath. If they worked together they could do this.

A few minutes later, she had everyone organized into an orderly line. She spoke to each in turn, assessing their needs and writing it all down in a notebook. It was too late to do any more that night, so Kit asked the costumes to come back again tomorrow.

When she finally got into bed, she felt completely exhausted but triumphant. Now that the news about Winifred and the nurse was spreading, she had a feeling that every mannequin in the museum would be begging for their help.

CHAPTER 13

'You don't look like you've had much kip,' said Bard the next morning, eyeing Kit over the top of his mug.

'I couldn't sleep,' said Kit, which was perfectly true. She didn't think he looked up to much, either. He was unshaven and his eyes were bloodshot and red-rimmed.

She took the mahogany-coloured tea that her grandfather pushed towards her. She'd drunk a lot of this since arriving at Moonstone. Odd to think that was only four days ago. So much had happened that it felt like weeks.

'Bard,' she said resolutely. 'I've made a decision and I need to tell you about it.'

'What's that, then?' he grunted.

'It's three weeks until the inspection and my dad won't be back from South America until the day before, which means I've got exactly two weeks and six days before I have to go home. It's not long, so I'm going to make a start straight away.'

'A start on what?'

'On . . . on clearing up Moonstone.'

Bard didn't laugh this time, he looked angry instead.

'Don't talk daft. I've told you already, it's a complete waste of time. What d'you think you can achieve in three weeks? You have no idea what you are talking about.'

'I don't care,' said Kit. 'It's better than doing nothing.'

'No it's not. You'd be better off going back to London.'

'I don't want to go back to London. I'm staying hear with you until Dad gets back.'

There was a long pause, while Bard glared down at the table and Kit looked out of the window.

'So . . . so you won't, won't help me, then?' she said at last in a small voice.

'No I will not. I've got more sense. If you want to spend the next few weeks working your socks off for no reason at all, then be my guest, but you'll be doing it on your own.'

'Fine,' said Kit pushing her chair violently back from the table and standing up. 'That's what I'll do, then.'

* * *

Ten minutes later she stood alone in the middle of the music salon feeling glum. There was so much wrong with the room. The ceiling was peeling, the musical instruments were filthy, the chandelier was swathed with cobwebs, the furniture was broken, the object labels were disintegrating, and the lights kept flickering on and off.

Kit nearly gave up there and then. What difference could she hope to make, even in this one, small gallery, let alone an entire museum? Then she remembered Fenella and Minna and all the others, and what would happen to them if Finn Scudder bought Moonstone, and she resolutely picked up a broom and got started.

This was the beginning of one of the hardest weeks of Kit's life. Awake for much of the night helping Fenella, she soon became exhausted, and it didn't help that her nightmare was worse than ever. She had little energy for her day-time cleaning work, but she kept going as best she could.

Progress was desperately slow. Occasionally a visitor came to the museum and would stop and stare, making Kit feel uncomfortable. Worse than this were the visits from Bard, who seemed to get a kick out of coming to see how badly she was doing. He would hang around in the doorway and shake his head in a pitying kind of way until she wanted to hit him.

At night, she had Lady Ann Hoops and Kiko Kai to contend with, and they were even worse. Kit was terrified of both of them, but she forced herself to try and make them see sense. For three nights in a row she went to them and attempted to explain the situation, but they wouldn't listen, averting their eyes, as if Kit was too repulsive to even look at, and sweeping off in opposite directions with their noses in the air.

Everyone else continued to follow their lead, although this didn't stop them coming up to the sewing room to be mended and cleaned. All Kit could do was smile at them encouragingly and try not to lose her temper.

In the meantime, the sewing work was progressing well. While Kit operated the Hoover, Fenella worked away with needle and thread, like someone possessed. Kit could see the desperate determination in her face and knew she was thinking of Minna. If patching and mending would help bring her beloved sister back, then nothing was going to stop her. She barely moved from the table and the mannequins flocked up the spiral stairs to see her. Kit had to allocate numbers to stop them bickering about whose turn it was next.

Then one evening, three nights after they had started work, something unexpected happened. Sir Jasper Stockings came to the sewing room to ask if anything could be done about Captains John's over-long sleeves.

'I've no idea,' said Kit feeling harassed. 'Go and tell him he needs to come up here in person.'

'Ah yes,' said Sir Jasper 'I'll let him know directly.' But he made no move to leave. He'd already had his replica stockings washed and his tattered lace cuffs mended and Kit was at a loss to know why he didn't go away again.

'I was wondering . . .' Sir Jasper said hesitantly. 'That is to say, might I take a turn with the facuum-prover?'

Kit was knocked for six. 'Are you offering to help us, Sir Jasper?'

'Well I suppose, if you put it like that . . . You won't mention it to Lady Ann, will you?'

'Why would I do that?' said Kit.

After that, she showed him how to use the

Hoover, making him practise on the window curtains.

'I say, this is fun,' said Sir Jasper as he held the hose, while Kit flicked dust off Tatyana Kozlov's traditional Russian folk costume. 'Damn it if I don't come back again tomorrow, young sir, and help you out.'

And he did. And not only that, but he brought along Ping Xing, the man in the Chinese dragon robe, as his assistant. Then, half an hour later, Claudia Clack appeared in the sewing room and offered to lend Fenella a hand with some of the stitching. Kit watched in astonishment as she tucked her handkerchief resolutely up her sleeve and settled down bedside Fenella with an actual smile on her face.

Once she was confident that Sir Jasper and Ping Xing knew what they were doing with the Hoover, Kit was free to go back to her work in the music salon. Standing on a chair, she was attempting to reach up to the chandelier with a broom, when Dorothy Dorsey, the woman in the green riding habit from the nineteenth century, suddenly walked into the room and ordered Kit to give her a job. Kit was so shocked, she nearly dropped the broom on her head.

'Help with the cleaning?' she asked in disbelief. 'But . . . but what if Kiko Kai catches you?'

Dorothy shrugged as if she didn't care very much if she did.

'Haven't had much experience with housework,' she admitted in a horsey voice. 'But I've mucked out a stable or two in my time, and how different can it be?'

Mindful of Dorothy's clothes, Kit made her an apron out of an old dust sheet and set her to work on the wood panelling.

'Not dissimilar to grooming a horse, is it?' remarked Dorothy patting the patch of wood she had been polishing for the last hour.

'You can probably move on to the next bit now,' suggested Kit, calculating that at this rate Dorothy would still be grooming the panels when the inspector arrived.

The following night, however, Dorothy brought along Tatyana Kozlov, the woman in the Russian folk costume. Tatyana came from a less privileged background than most of the inhabitants of Moonstone and knew far more about cleaning than Kit. She didn't say much and smiled even less, but she was practical and strong and knew what to do.

At last Kit felt they were making some headway in the museum. Bard must have noticed a difference too, because he began to look baffled rather than pitying when he came to watch her progress. On one occasion she caught him down in the library, staring in perplexity at the now visible blood stains on the nurse's skirt. He scratched his head, but moved off quickly when he saw Kit watching.

Another time she spotted him in the oriental room, eyeballing Captain John's sleeves, which had mysteriously ruched themselves neatly up his arms. He caught sight of Kit behind him in one of the mirrors, but this time he didn't walk away and turned on her angrily.

'Have you been mucking around with this costume?' he demanded.

'Only . . . only to sort out his sleeves,' said Kit, 'They were getting damaged, dangling down like that.'

'Damaged?' he repeated as if he couldn't believe his ears. 'D'you not remember what I told you would happen to these costumes when Finn Scudder buys this place? This garment will be cinders in a month. You think pushing his sleeves up is going to make any difference? Nothing you do is going to save Moonstone.'

And with that, he walked out of the room, leaving Kit feeling devastated all over again. Bard was right. What a fool she had been to think she could change anything. Even with the help of Tatyana and the others, it wasn't going to be enough.

On a plinth, close by, stood Kiko Kai. Kit looked up at the mannequin in the kimono. 'Please,' she whispered, 'Please change your mind. It's our only hope.' But the stony face of the mannequin stared into the distance, as cold and indifferent as always. There was something about her expression that made Kit feel suddenly belligerent. She thought of Fenella, working away doggedly, night after night. For their sake, if for no one else's, she would not give up yet.

* * *

By the end of the sixth night, they had finally finished the music salon and moved into the Rabology room. Kit tried to stay positive, but the new gallery was a grim sight and she felt tired just looking at it. She sighed and bent down wearily to pick up a piece of paper from under a chair, glancing at it indifferently. She paused. She'd seen it before. It was the plan of Moonstone Manor that that Finn Scudder had brought with him on the day that Graham Groid had visited.

Kit studied it for a moment. It reminded her of her mum's map of Moonstone, but it looked a lot older. She found a date—1705—well over three hundred years ago. This predated the time when Fenella and Minna Silk-Hatton had lived at Moonstone by about fifty years. The rooms were labelled just like Emmie's map, but the writing was old-fashioned and the names were different. The portrait gallery for instance, was known in the past as 'the vestibule' and the summer room was called 'the grand parlour'.

She traced a finger around the perimeter of the gallery, thinking of Minna trapped inside. She imagined the forlorn little figure, in the vast wallpapered room, whimpering with fear. She knew what it felt like because she had lived this experience night after night in her own nightmare.

She had nearly completed the circle when her finger stopped. She peered more closely. There was something odd here. Was that a door in the east wall? But that couldn't be right. The only way into the summer room was from the portrait gallery, so what door was this? It opened into what was now the boudoir, and Kit's heart suddenly began to beat faster. That huge bed, which filled most of the room, anything could be hidden behind it. Perhaps the door was still there?

CHAPTER 14

With the map crushed in one hand, Kit started to run.

'Has something happened?' called Dorothy after her. 'Where are you going?'

'To the boudoir,' shouted Kit. 'Tell Fenella . . . Think I've found a way into the summer room . . . Rescue Minna.' She couldn't stop and explain anymore and hurtled off through the galleries.

Her brain worked fast. There were a few things she must collect from the flat, before going to the four-poster room. When she got there she headed straight for the kitchen and, not troubling to keep the noise down, she wrenched open Bard's odds and ends drawer, scattering the contents on the floor. Right at the back she found what she was looking for, a small, old-fashioned torch, a candle in a foil holder, and a box of matches.

A moment later, she was up in her bedroom, extracting a clean bed sheet from the chest of drawers. She was half way down the stairs again when she thought of something else. Returning to her room, she reached behind the curtains and pulled out the walking stick she had threatened Captain John with on the day she had first met Fenella. It had a hook at one end and might come in handy.

There was no sign of Fenella in the boudoir when Kit arrived there a few minutes later. She had not been inside this room since she first looked around the museum, and had forgotten how colossal the bed was. It filled most of the space and each carved post was as big as a grandfather clock. The huge headboard was pushed up hard against the wall that separated the boudoir from the summer room. There was only one way to find out if the doorway was still there. She was going to have to crawl underneath.

She lifted one corner of the heavy counterpane and noticed that the frame of the bed was unusually low. It wasn't going to be much fun crawling under there. She took out the torch and shone the light into the darkness. It looked as if about three hundred years of filth were under that bed. The floor was thick with sticky dust and there were countless cobwebs dangling down form the worm-eaten slats. Kit thought about all the spiders that must be living under there and began to dread the task that lay ahead. But what choice did she have? She was the only person at Moonstone who could do this job, and thinking about it wasn't going to make it any easier. She was wearing a small apron and she removed it and tied it over her head like a bonnet. At least that might keep the worst of the spiders out of her hair. Then, dumping the sheet on the counterpane, she lay down on the floor and began to wriggle under the bed.

It was one of the worst things she'd ever done. The bed wasn't high enough for her to crawl properly, so she had to squirm on her belly in the filth, pulling herself along with her arms, dragging the walking stick with her. Kit could feel her heart pounding in her chest as she struggled to catch her breath. Cobwebs brushed her face and when she tried to sweep them away something crawled across her hand. She squeaked in horror and knocked it off. Then, as if this wasn't bad enough, she heard a scuttling sound and realized that it wasn't only spiders that she had to worry about. There must be mice under here too, or even worse, rats.

Kit felt panic rising inside her and she banged the stick on the floor, hard, to frighten the rodents away. Then she shut her eyes and forced herself to keep going. At last her fingers touched something solid ahead. With great difficulty she extracted the torch from her pocket and switched on the light again. Thank goodness, there was the wall at last. She could see the wood panelling stretching away, on either side, but in the centre, there was a slight recess. Could that be a doorway? It was impossible to tell from where she was lying. Kit snaked sideways until her head was more or less in the alcove, then she repositioned the torch, pointing it upwards. The light flooded the wall, and rolling over to look, Kit could see high above her the distinctive shape of a door handle.

She smiled in the darkness. She'd found it, but it was too soon to celebrate. She had to get the door open first. This was where the walking stick came in, but even getting it from a horizontal to a vertical position was tricky. She managed it in the end by swinging it up between the tiny gap that separated the wall and the bed. Now she had to hook the end of the walking stick over the door handle so that she could pull it down.

The stick knocked and crashed against the door. Several times it caught on the handle and she pulled, but the door didn't budge.

Kit tried again and again. Her arms felt weak and wobbly from the strain of holding up the stick and her knuckles bashed against the wall painfully with each swing. The frustration was mounting and Kit wondered how much longer she could keep going. Furiously, she lunged one more time and pushed violently against the wood with her head.

'Move, will you,' she shouted in desperation. This time, something happened. The handle seemed to depress further and, at the same moment, she felt the wood shift. The door had given way at last.

A draft of air filtered out of the gap. Kit dropped the stick and pushed at the bottom of the door. It moved with heavy slowness, as if it had not been opened for many years. Soon it was wide enough for Kit to wriggle through and she stood up.

The weak beam of light from her torch did not reach far, but she sensed that she was in a big space. She felt in her back pocket for the candle, scrabbled with the matches and lit the wick. The gallery flickered into view and immediately she recognized the flower pattern on the walls. She had seen it before in her doll's house. This was the room from her nightmare.

With the candle in one hand and the torch in the other, she moved slowly through the room, searching for signs of the little girl. She felt the same claustrophobic sense of panic she had in her dream and the unbearable desire to turn around and go back through the door to safety.

'Minna,' she called softly, but there was no answer.

Kit began to wonder if she had made a ghastly mistake. What if she had got it all wrong? What if her nightmare was just a random coincidence and she had built up Fenella's hopes for nothing? The thought of the heartbreak she would inflict, if this turned out to be the case, was terrible and Kit's search became more feverish. Her footsteps echoed behind her as she rushed from one end of the gallery to the other.

'Minna, where are you? Minna!'

She stopped for a moment, listening. Was that the sound of tiny breaths she could hear, or was she imagining it? She tiptoed closer towards a pair of heavy, floor-length curtains and pulled one back. Then she stifled a cry and, dropped her torch with a clatter, for there, curled up on the window seat and sleeping soundly, was little Minna.

Tears of relief filled Kit's eyes. She bent over the small figure dressed in a tiny bodice and skirt and, with one finger, stroked her fuzzy curls. She had never even seen Minna before and yet there was an undeniable connection between them. She imagined what it must have been like for her, trapped in this room as the fire raged outside. Kit had lived through the nightmare often enough to know how terrifying it was and she wept for Minna now.

'Don't worry, little one. I'm going to get your sister,' she whispered to the sleeping figure before creeping back to the door.

Crawling under the bed was no problem now. She thought only of Minna as she battled her way back to the bedroom.

'Fenella,' she cried, as she emerged into the boudoir. 'Fenella I've found her, I've found Minna!'

But Fenella wasn't there. Instead, most of the inhabitants of Moonstone seemed to be waiting for her. They were crammed into the tiny space around the bed and those that couldn't fit were just outside the door. As Kit struggled to her feet, she spotted the menacing forms of Kiko Kai and Lady Ann Hoops in the entrance. Something in the way that they were both glaring at her made her glance down at her clothes, and she realized that she was covered from head to toe in dirt. She could only imagine what she must look like, with an apron tied over her head, but then she remembered why she was so filthy and stared back at them defiantly.

Just then there was a movement behind the imposing figures of Lady Ann Hopps and Kiko Kai, and Kit glimpsed Fenella struggling to get through. Without hesitation, the girl forced her way between the formidable pair, completely oblivious to their exclamations of outrage. She only had eyes for Kit and, when she reached her, she fastened cold fingers around her wrist.

'She's all right,' said Kit, eager to reassure her. 'I've seen her. She's asleep in the summer room, but I need you to come with me to get her. Minna doesn't know me and I don't want to frighten her.'

Fenella nodded. Kit picked up the sheet she had brought with her and began unfolding it.

Kiko Kai elbowed her way through the crowd. She lifted the counterpane on the bed and peered underneath.

'You must be out of your senses,' she said. 'It's none of my concern, but if you ask her to crawl through all that dirt, she will be ruined forever.'

This was such a stupid thing to say that Kit decided to ignore it. Did Kiko really think she would endanger the condition of her best friend? She laid the sheet on the floor as best she could in the limited space.

'Do you trust me?' she said to Fenella.

Fenella's face was apprehensive, but she nodded decisively.

'Then lie on the sheet. I'll wrap you up in it and pull you into the room.'

Kiko let out a little shriek.

'Let me through,' boomed a voice from the doorway. 'Fenella! Get up off the floor this instant. What shockingly unladylike behaviour.'

But Fenella didn't get up. Instead she crossed her arms over her front and smiled up at Kit.

'How dare you disobey me!' cried Lady Ann furiously. 'You cannot trust a thing this child says. Look at the state of her. Do you want to end up looking like that? Let me through, I say.'

But nobody budged. Was it Kit's imagination or did they draw, ever so slightly, closer together? Either way, the size of Lady Ann's skirt made it impossible for her to do anything about it.

'Are you ready?' said Kit, looking down at her friend, who was now wrapped up like a mummy.

Fenella nodded once more and Kit took hold

of the loose end of the sheet.

'Right then, here we go.'

If it had been difficult lugging a walking stick under the bed, this was ten times worse. Even though Fenella was small and light, the weight inside the sheet felt impossibly heavy to poor Kit, who had to haul it along while lying on her tummy. Inch by inch she dragged Fenella closer to the hidden door. They reached it at last and Kit let go of the sheet and crawled through the entrance. Now she could stand up and, reaching back, she pulled Fenella through the door in one fluid movement. In a moment her friend was on her feet beside her in the summer room.

The candle was still flickering where Kit had left it and she led the way quickly to the window seat. There was a sound of flying feet and a rustle of skirts as Fenella rushed past her.

'Minna. My Minna,' she said in a sweet, husky voice.

Kit's jaw dropped. It was the first time she had ever heard Fenella speak.

The little figure on the seat stirred and opened her eyes. Seeing her sister, Minna cried out and held out both her arms. Fenella swept her up and held her tightly as if she would never let go.

Kit's cheeks were wet again. Over Fenella's

shoulder, a pair of solemn eyes were gazing straight back at her and Kit gave a watery smile. Minna stretched out a chubby hand towards her.

'Emmie?'

Kit felt as if all the breadth had been knocked out of her. She stepped back and Minna's face clouded with sudden confusion. Kit was reeling. Did this mean what she thought it meant? She watched as Fenella put her sister gently on the floor and, holding her by the hand, led her forward.

Kit squatted down to Minna's level.

'I'm Kit,' she said firmly, removing the apron from her head, so that the child could see her properly. 'I'm Emmie's daught . . . I'm a friend of Emmie's.'

. . .

Ten minutes later, Kit reappeared in the boudoir dragging the sheet behind her. This time, there were two figures wrapped up in it, and as Minna's face came into view a great shout went up and they were immediately engulfed. Many hands reached down to help and soon they were all on their feet and Kit was being patted on the back and thanked by anyone who could reach her.

'Enough,' cried Lady Ann Hoops furiously. 'You should be ashamed of yourselves! How dare you be grateful to the likes of her? Why she is nothing but a menial servant girl who scrubs the floors. We would have found Minna in the end, without any help from her.'

Kit swung round and stared disbelievingly at Lady Ann. There was something about her stubborn refusal to recognize what Kit had just done that reminded her of Sir Henry, and it made her see red. She looked directly at the formidable figure and shouted, 'Then you would have found her too late.'

You could have heard a pin drop, but Kit hadn't finished yet, in fact she had only just begun. She pushed her way roughly through the crowd and sprang up onto the low window sill. Ignoring Lady Ann Hoops, she turned to face the rest of the crowd. This time she was determined to make them listen.

'It might still be too late for all of you, unless you bury your pride and start helping to save Moonstone.' Her voice was strong and clear, without any hint of a wobble. 'It's not just your home that's at risk,' she went on, 'your actual lives depend on it. Do you know what's going to happen to you if the museum is sold? You'll be rubbish set for the dump! And that's if you're lucky. They might decide to chuck you on a bonfire, and there would be nothing you could do about it. Now do you understand how serious this is?'

There were agitated movements from the crowd. Everyone suddenly looked shocked and frightened.

'It's not over yet,' Kit said more gently. 'We can still turn this around, but you've got to trust me. I've just rescued Minna for you, haven't I? I'm sure I can help you too, but I can't do it on my own.' She paused and her eyes travelled around the room. 'It's time for all of you to stop this pointless bickering between the centuries and to unite once and for all.'

Kit stopped, feeling suddenly exhausted. The crowd looked back at her, stony faced. Had she failed yet again? She closed her eyes in despair. And then, over in the corner of the room, someone started to clap. Kit's eyes opened in surprise and saw that it was Tatyana Kozlov. Before she could blink, Dorothy Dorsey had begun to clap too and, after a slight pause, Nurse Butcher, Winifred Ware and Sir Jasper Stockings had joined in. Soon others were following suit—the two gentlemen in dressing gowns, the woman in the Indian sari, the ballet dancer, the African warrior, the lady with the bicycle and, before she knew it, almost everyone in the room was clapping enthusiastically, and

Fenella and Minna were hugging her, and Kit was blushing and smiling and feeling that this was probably one of the best moments of her life.

There were only two people who did not participate—Lady Ann Hoops and Kiko Kai. They looked on with utter disdain before turning on their heels and storming off in opposite directions.

CHAPTER 15

Kit woke up in the morning feeling refreshed and euphoric, after the best night's sleep she'd had in weeks. She had not been troubled once by her nightmare, and hoped that now Minna had been found she would never be haunted by the dream again.

Kit immediately started to formulate plans. There were exactly fifteen days left before her dad returned from South America, and the inspection itself was due to take place just one day after that. It wasn't long, but with so many to help, a lot could be achieved. Kit had to admit that, with the exception of Tatyana, no one had much experience and most of them seemed hopelessly unpractical, but she was sure that they would get the hang of things soon enough. She would need to allocate the jobs sensibly and make sure everyone knew what they were doing. She grabbed a pad of paper and started making lists.

Soon she had drawn up a complicated timetable, complete with dates, locations and notes. Without realizing it she seemed to have recreated one of Sir Henry's itineraries. She pulled a face. Maybe she took after her dad in more ways than she knew.

Planning a programme for a large team of workers turned out to be a time-consuming job, and Kit spent most of the day sitting at the table in her room, poring over her mum's map and trying to make sure that she hadn't forgotten anything. As well as all the galleries, many of the costumes still required repair work and she had to make sure there was enough time to fit this in as well.

'Given up, then?' said Bard scathingly when Kit joined him for an eggs on toast dinner.

'Given up what?'

'Fixing up the museum all on your own.'

'Nope,' said Kit. 'I'm just taking some time out to make a plan of action.'

Bard frowned and blew on his tea. 'Wish you hadn't set your heart so much on saving

Moonstone,' he muttered. 'It'll only upset you when it all goes wrong. You're like your mum, you are.'

'Am I?' said Kit. The mention of her mother made her think of Minna and the shock of that single word she had spoken in the summer room last night—Emmie.

Just then the phone rang in the office and Bard got up to answer it. For a moment Kit was distracted and looked after him uneasily. What if it was the council? Maybe they wanted to change the date of the inspection? Then she remembered how late it was. They would never call Bard at this time in the evening.

It must have been a long phone call because Bard did not reappear again. Kit washed up and escaped back upstairs. She was thinking about the importance of garment protection. It was no good getting everyone to help clean up the museum if they damaged their own costumes in the process. They must wear aprons and she tried to work out how many meters of fabric they would need to make one for ever outfit in the museum. She could do with a calculator for this and immediately thought of the one on her phone.

But where was her phone? She hadn't used it for days. Then she remembered zipping it into the pocket on her back pack during her drive back from Axly with Bard. It didn't take her long to find. She switched it on and was waiting impatiently for it to come to life when it suddenly began to ring.

'Hello,' she said vaguely, her mind still on fabric calculations

Someone seemed to be shouting on the other end of the phone. Kit suddenly came upright in her chair. In a flash she had forgotten all about aprons.

'. . . AND NO IDEA WHERE YOU WERE. WE HAVE BEEN WORRIED SICK. YOU'VE BEEN GONE MORE THAN A WEEK. HOW COULD YOU BE SO SELFISH? I THOUGHT WE WOULD NEVER FIND YOU. I THOUGHT WE'D LOST YOU FOREVER.' There was a sudden sobbing sound, as if the person who was yelling was also crying.

'Er, is that you, Roz?' said Kit.

'AND ALL THAT RUBBISH YOU MADE UP ON THE PHONE. JUST LIES. I CAN NEVER, NEVER TRUST YOU AGAIN.'

'Roz, I'm so sorry. I never meant you to worry. I didn't think you'd find out that I was gone.'

'NOT FIND OUT! DON'T YOU THINK ALBERT AND I EVER SPEAK TO EACH

OTHER?'

'Well you don't often—'

'AND EVEN THEN WE DIDN'T KNOW WHERE YOU WERE. IT TOOK US AGES TO FIND THAT NOTE YOU LEFT FOR DAD.'

'Oh, so that's how you tracked me down.'

'I CANNOT BEGIN TO DESCRIBE HOW ANGRY AL IS. I'VE NEVER SEEN HIM LIKE THIS. YOU'LL BE LUCKY IF HE EVER SPEAKS TO YOU AGAIN. AND I DON'T EVEN WANT TO THINK ABOUT WHAT DAD IS GOING TO SAY WHEN HE HEARS ABOUT IT.'

'You're going to tell him?'

'OF COURSE I'M GOING TO TELL HIM.'

'Roz, you've got to listen to me—' began Kit.

'NO, YOU LISTEN TO ME, KATHERINE HALLIWELL. I'M DRIVING UP TO MOONSTONE TOMORROW TO GET YOU. AND YOU'D BETTER BE READY WHEN I GET THERE.'

'But Roz I can't go home at the moment. Roz, please. There's something I've got to do . . .'

But there was silence on the other end of the phone and Kit knew that she had been cut her off.

She stared numbly out of the window. The

call had lasted less than a minute. How could everything fall apart in such a short space of time? She was still sitting in the same chair, still holding the same pen. The ink from the last word she had written was barely dry, and yet everything had changed.

Her bedroom door creaked. Kit turned to look and saw her grandfather standing there. One glance at his face made it clear that he knew what was going on. Then she remembered the call he had taken in his office, just minutes before her own phone had rung.

'So it was all a lie, was it,' said Bard. 'All that stuff you said about sending your dad a message and letting him know where you were? You just made it up?'

'I did send him a message,' said Kit dully. 'I told him I was at Moonstone, but he . . . he doesn't always have time to read the things I write.'

'Doesn't always have time? You mean you were counting on it. Thought you'd take me for a ride, did you? Pull the wool over my eyes. What an old fool you must have thought I was for believing you. Probably had a good laugh about it, did you?'

'No, I didn't,' said Kit. 'It wasn't like that at all.'

'It was my one condition—tell your family where you are. That's all I asked. D'you realize how much hot water you could get me in for this? Your father won't believe I had nothing to do with it. I'll have Sir Henry blasted Halliwell accusing me of aiding and abetting you.'

'No he won't. I'll tell him it was nothing to do with you.'

'Oh, well that's OK, then,' said Bard sarcastically. 'He's really going to believe anything you've got to say after all the lies you've told.'

'Well, what would you have done in my place?' said Kit, her temper beginning to rise. 'I had to get away. You don't understand what it's like at home. I don't fit in. Everyone thinks I'm such a nuisance. My dad is embarrassed of me.'

'Oh, don't talk nonsense,' said Bard.

'It isn't nonsense,' said Kit. 'It was one of the last things he said to me before he left—you're an embarrassment. Those where his exact words.'

'Well I'm sure he didn't mean it like that.'

'Yes he did,' insisted Kit. 'He's ashamed of me because I'm not clever like Roz and Al and because I failed the entrance exam for the stupid school he wants me to go to. That's why I ran away.'

'Well running away isn't a solution for anything,' said Bard. 'You've got to face up to your troubles.'

Kit's jaw dropped. 'I can't believe you can say that with a straight face.'

'What d'you mean?' he said defensively.

'You actually need me to spell it out for you?' said Kit incredulously, all her pent up frustration at his recent behaviour coming to a sudden head. 'You haven't done a very good job of facing up to your troubles this week, have you? Sitting around all day, feeling sorry for yourself and then laughing at me for trying to save Moonstone because you've given up.'

'But I told you, there's no point trying to save it.'

'Yes there is,' shouted Kit. 'You just can't be bothered. You gave up looking after Moonstone years ago, ever since the day my mum left.'

'How dare you talk to me like that?' said Bard, now nearly as angry as Kit. 'You have no right to pass judgement on things you don't understand. What was I supposed to do? She knew I couldn't manage without her.'

'Then why did she go?' demanded Kit and this was the question that had been haunting her ever since last night, when she had discovered that her mum had known Minna and Fenella.

'She fell in love with your dad,' said Bard. 'That's why she went.'

But Kit shook her head. 'There's more to it than that. What happened before my dad came along? Did you drive her away, just like you're trying to do to me?'

Kit stopped to brush away some angry tears. She knew she had gone too far. The old man was silent and when she dared raise her eyes, she saw that his expression had changed. He looked stricken. He lowered himself slowly onto the bed. Then he took out his familiar, filthy handkerchief and blew his nose.

'You're right,' he said in a low voice. 'It was my fault she left. It wasn't easy when her mum died, but we managed for a few years, just the two of us. She was only fourteen when Katherine got ill, still a child, and I expected so much of her.

'I knew I wasn't a great dad and I didn't know how to tell her that I loved her, so I tried to show her in other ways. Started making her this big old doll's house. Took me years to finish. I modelled it on Moonstone, made miniature versions of all her favourite rooms in the museum. She was too old to play with it, of course, but it was my way of showing her that I cared. All the love I had for her went into that house. If I was bad tempered, or feeling lost, I'd work on the doll's house, when I should have been spending time with my girl.' Bard shook his head miserably. 'And then all these years later, you came along, turned the place topsy-turvy, and it was almost like I had my Emmie back again, only you're not Emmie, are you.'

Kit watched numbly as Bard stood up stiffly and shuffled over to the door. His shoulders were bent and he looked old and tired. His last words had hurt her deeply. As usual she wasn't good enough and she felt rejected, but it didn't make any difference to what she had to say now.

'My mum kept it,' she said.

'What?'

'She kept the doll's house. My brother and sister always said it was one of her most treasured possessions. It's in my room now.'

The old man stood frozen in the doorway and for a moment, he looked as if he wanted to say something. Then, without another word, he turned and walked out of the room, closing the door softly behind him.

CHAPTER 16

Kit opened her eyes. She was lying on her bed, fully clothed, with a feeling of wretchedness heavy inside her. She couldn't think why this was, and then it all came back to her. The phone call from her sister, the awful argument with Bard and, worst of all, the fact that she would be leaving Moonstone forever.

Kit suddenly became aware that it was light. More than that, there was sunshine pouring through her window. She seized her watch from the bedside table. It couldn't be eight a.m.—she had slept the entire night away. She must have been so exhausted from the shock, and upset, and the many sleepless nights that she had dropped off by mistake. Kit flopped back onto the bed and stared in despair at the cracked ceiling. Why hadn't Fenella come by and woken her? Perhaps she thought she needed the rest? Without meaning to, Kit had thrown away her last chance to see everyone and explain. She wouldn't even get an opportunity to say goodbye. Tears of hopelessness began to slide down her cheeks and into her hair.

With clumsy fingers and swollen eyes, Kit packed up her belongings, squashing them into her backpack any-old-how. Her room looked stripped and forlorn when she had finished and she wondered who would be the next person to stay there. Maybe one of Finn Scudder's horrible conference guests. The thought was like torture to her, and she picked up the itinerary she had made yesterday and escaped down the attic stairs.

Stumbling along the passage to the museum, she knew that what she was about to do was pointless, but it wasn't going to stop her. How could she leave Moonstone without seeing her friends one last time, even if they couldn't see her? Slowly she made her way from gallery to gallery, whispering her farewells.

Up in the store she was nearly overwhelmed by the many familiar faces.

'Don't give up,' she whispered to Tatyana Kozlov. She folded the itinerary she had brought with her and slid it between the finger and thumb of the mannequin. It was the only thing left that she could do for them now and she hurried from the room, not looking back.

Last of all she went to the nursery. In spite of everything she smiled as she came through the door, and saw Fenella and Minna standing on a plinth side by side. They looked so happy together. But then Kit remembered what was going to happen to them if the council sold Moonstone, and a wave of despair swept over her. She battled against it, dashing the tears away with the back of her hand.

'I'm so sorry that I've let you down. They are making me leave Moonstone. You must do everything you can to save this place,' she whispered. 'I won't ever forget you.' Kit kissed Fenella lightly on the cheek and touched her cold hand one last time.

* * *

Rosalind arrived much sooner than she had expected. Kit was waiting outside and she watched the car's slow, bumpy approach down the drive. As it got closer, Kit realized that her brother had come too. He was sitting in the passenger seat, and he had a face like thunder.

Her mouth went dry. She was completely unprepared for this development and it was all she could do to stop herself from running off to hide.

The car pulled up a few feet away, but nobody got out. Kit could see through the window that Roz was crying and Albert was trying to comfort her. It was an awful sight and Kit's throat began to ache painfully. Would her brother and sister ever forgive her? She thought about all the things that they had done for her over the years, how they had helped look after her, from when they were only teenagers. It must have been difficult for them always having a younger kid around, and yet they had never complained. She thought of Fenella's care and love for Minna; maybe her own siblings had not been so different after all.

At last Albert opened the car door and got out. He looked at Kit coldly. 'I hope you're ready to leave,' he said. 'Can you go and get your things.'

'Is . . . is Roz all right?'

'Does she look all right to you?'

Kit shook her head slightly. 'I'm really, really sorry, Al.'

'Well, it's a bit late for that. Go on, get your things. We want to be out of here as soon as possible. This place doesn't have great memories for Roz and me.'

'You've been here before?' said Kit in surprise.

'We used to come occasionally with Mum, years ago.'

'I didn't know,' said Kit. 'Why didn't you ever—'

'Look, can you just get your things.'

'Al,' said a voice and Rosalind emerged from the car. Her eyes were red-rimmed and she had a tissue in one hand. 'Look who's here.' She nodded towards the house.

'Oh great, this is all we need,' said Albert.

Kit turned to see who they were talking about and saw Bard walking towards them across the gravel.

'I don't want to see him,' hissed Roz.

'Well, thanks to Kit, it doesn't look like we've got much choice,' muttered Albert.

Kit stared blankly from her brother to her sister. What exactly was going on here? She dug her nails into the palm of her hand and watched apprehensively as the old man approached. Then she frowned. What had happened to Bard? He looked different. He was swinging his arms as he came towards them, in an unusually energetic way and he looked almost happy, as if a great weight had been removed. Was he that pleased to see the back of her?

When he finally reached them he didn't even look at Kit, but nodded pleasantly at Albert and Rosalind. 'Well you've both grown since I saw you last.'

This was greeted with a stony silence.

'How old would you have been then,' went on Bard. 'Bout sixteen, seventeen?'

'I was thirteen and Roz was eleven,' said Albert icily.

'That young, eh? Same sort of age as your sister Kit is now.'

'Yes, I suppose so.'

'If you don't mind,' said Bard after slight pause, 'There's a few things I'd like to say about her before you go.'

Kit covered her face with her hands in shame. She knew what was coming. He was going to tell them about the row they'd had last night and the unforgivable things she'd said. To have her behaviour discussed in front of her like this was nearly more than she could bear.

'She's not your standard twelve-year-old kid, is she? D'you want to know how she got here? Took a bus from London, then walked all the way from Axly. Ten miles it is. Should have realized then that she was going to be a trouble maker.'

Kit screwed up her face inside her hands, and tried to prepare herself.

'The worst thing about her is that she can't stop herself from meddling. Haven't had a day's peace since she got here. But in spite of all that, I can't tell you how glad I am that she came.'

Kit stared at Bard through the gap between her fingers. Was he being sarcastic?

'I don't know how I would have got through the last week without her. See, the council want to take Moonstone away from me. I've let it fall into bad repair over the last few years and now they're thinking to sell it to some idiot who wants to turn it into a conference centre. They're sending an inspector round in a couple of weeks to make the final decision.'

Bard sighed. His eyes were still fixed on Albert and Rosalind.

'I was ready to pack it in but Kit refused to give up on Moonstone. I've watched her put everything into turning the place around. She's worked night and day. Like your mum, she is, stubborn and brave and determined, and d'you know what I did? I laughed at her for trying.'

Up until this point, Bard hadn't looked once at Kit but now he turned towards her and smiled painfully. 'You were right in what you said about me last night. I was a lousy dad to Emmie and I've been a lousy grandfather to you and all. I'm sorry.'

Kit couldn't speak.

'If it's not too late, I want to try and make it up to you. I want to give your idea a go, see if we can't save Moonstone and send Finn blasted Scudder packing once and for all. Would you stay and let me help you?'

He turned to Albert and Rosalind. 'And I would be honoured if you would stop here and lend a hand too?'

Kit's eyes flicked in the direction of her brother and sister. Roz was pressing her lips together uncertainly but Albert looked furious.

'I don't believe I'm hearing this,' he said. 'You seriously expect Roz and me to stay and help, after what you did to us?'

'What do you mean?' asked Bard.

'You abandoned us when we were kids! Our mum had just died and you walked out of our lives without a backwards glance. We never heard from you again. Roz even wrote, begging you to come and see us. You never even bothered to answer her letter.'

'I thought it was for the best,' said Bard, his voice full of anguish. 'There was nothing I wanted more than to see you and your sisters, but your dad and I couldn't stand the sight of each other, and with your mum gone, I thought it would be easier for you if I kept away.'

'Well, it wasn't,' shouted Albert.

'I was wrong,' said Bard. 'And I am more sorry than you will ever know.' He rubbed his head with a hand. 'Seem to have got so many things wrong in my life. But Kit's made me see that it's not too late to change things now. Why don't you stay? Stay and help save Moonstone. If not for my sake, then for Kit's.'

There were tears sliding down Roz's cheeks again, but Kit understood now that they weren't about her. This went a lot further back than that. Her brother and sister exchanged glances.

'What do you think, Al,' whispered Roz and Kit could tell by her voice that she was actually considering Bard's suggestion. She waited, hardly able to breath.

Albert put an arm around his sister and shook his head. 'It's too late Roz. We can't change what's happened to us in the past.'

'No,' said Rosalind, blotting her eyes with the lump of wet tissue. 'You're right, but maybe we can change what happens in the future for Kit. She doesn't have to live the same life that we did. She isn't like us, Al. She's good at different things. Maybe Moonstone is just what she needs. I think Mum would want us to stay.'

Albert's feet ground restlessly in the gravel.

'All right,' he said at last, 'If that's what you two want, we'll stay.'

'Albert,' shrieked Kit. 'Do you mean it?'

He shrugged. 'I'm due a holiday. Haven't had one in five years.'

'And what about you, Roz. You can't take time off, can you? Your job is much too important.'

'If Al can take a break, I suppose I can too.'

Bard coughed. 'If you're going to help us try and put the museum back together, I'm not sure "break" is quite the right word for it. Moonstone's in a hell of a muddle I'm afraid.'

'I'm always up for a challenge,' said Albert.

'Good. Then I think there's one thing we all need to agree on—Kit's in charge,' said Bard firmly, 'It was her idea in the first place, so what she says, goes.'

Kit felt herself blush. 'Oh no, I don't want to—'

'That's fine by me,' said Roz.

'It'll make a nice change not to be the boss for once,' agreed Albert.

'But I—' began Kit.

'Well, that's settled then,' said Bard. 'Come on, let's go back indoors. Kit can run through

the plan and we'll have some more breakfast.
There's plenty of bread in the bin for toast.'

CHAPTER 17

'I've had a go tidying up in this room,' said Kit, leading her family into the music salon. She felt nervous showing them, as if they were about to judge a piece of her homework. 'I know it's not perfect, but it is better than it was.'

There was silence as everyone gazed around the room, critically.

'Well I can see you've done a lot of work,' said Albert. 'It's a shame about the ceiling though.'

'It needs repainting,' said Kit, feeling deflated.

'Well I can do that,' said Bard. 'Got a tall ladder down in the maintenance cupboard. I'll see to the broken furniture, too.'

Kit smiled at him gratefully.

'And what about all these flickering lights?' said Albert. 'It's a bit off-putting.'

'They've been on the blink for a while,' said Bard, avoiding eye contact. 'I've fixed them a few times but they soon go wrong again. Thing is, I caused a fire not so long ago, nearly burnt the place down, and I haven't dared go near any wiring since. 'Lectrics have never been my strong point.'

'Oh, is that how the fire started,' murmured Kit. 'Al, you're good at this kind of thing. Would you mind trying to sort out the lights?'

'Sure,' he said. 'I'd be happy to.' He was already fiddling with one of the bulbs.

'What about me, Kit? What can I do to help?' said Roz.

Kit's eyes darted around the room. 'I wonder if you could do something about the object labels?'

'What, these?' said Roz, bending down to pick up a particularly dilapidated example. 'I can't even read it.'

'Yes,' said Kit. 'That's kind of the problem.'

'How many are there do you think?'

'Oh, I don't know,' said Kit vaguely. 'Probably about two hundred.'

Albert started to laugh. 'Off you go then, Roz.

No pressure. Being a high-powered political advisor will feel like a piece of cake after this!'

They walked slowly on through the rest of the museum.

'So how long have we actually got?' asked her brother, eyeing the filthy bookshelves in the library.

'The inspection is exactly two weeks today,' said Kit.

Albert whistled. 'We'd better get started then.'

At least the costumes don't look too bad,' said Roz, gazing at the nurse. 'This one is surprisingly clean. She hasn't got a speck of dust on her.'

'No,' said Bard drily, looking at Kit. 'Odd that.'

Kit blushed and suggested they go outside to inspect the grounds.

* * *

From that moment on, everything changed at Moonstone. It wasn't only that the galleries now rang with unfamiliar noises—bangs and crashes, cheerful whistling, scraps of conversations, even a radio blaring—it was something else that had transformed the old place. Kit tried to work out what it was, and came to the conclusion that it must be hope.

Everyone threw themselves into the work and it was amazing how quickly it felt normal for them all to be there. Kit barely thought twice when she came into the kitchen and found Roz sitting at the table sorting through a huge heap of object labels.

'How's it going?' asked Kit.

'Challenging,' replied Roz. 'I've decided to scrap these completely. They're beyond saving.'

'What can we do instead though? We can't have a museum with no object labels.'

Roz held up a hand. 'Here's my plan. First I'm going to transcribe the old ones onto my lap top, then I'm going to redesign the lettering and layout and after that I'll get them professionally printed.'

'Oh I don't think Bard will be able to afford that,' said Kit quickly.

'I'm going to pay for it,' said Roz firmly. 'I know someone who runs a print design company. He'll give me a good deal and it won't be anything fancy.' Suddenly she looked nervous. 'You will have a look at my designs, won't you, Kit? I've never done anything like this before.'

Kit grinned and felt a warm glow inside her. Rosalind—her successful and intelligent big sister—was asking her for help.

Meanwhile Albert had more or less taken the entire museum lighting system to pieces. There were floorboards up all over Moonstone and wires everywhere.

'Is it safe what you're doing?' asked Kit uneasily, picking up a page of wiring diagrams that Albert had downloaded from the internet.

'Don't worry Kit, I'm sure I can work it out. It's not rocket science, and I was quite good at that.' A bell suddenly jangled. 'What's that awful noise?'

'It must be the visitor bell,' said Kit. 'And Bard's out working in the grounds. Do you think I should go down and speak to whoever they are? What shall I say?'

'I'm sure you'll think of something,' said Albert. 'You've always been good at handling people.'

'No I haven't,' said Kit, startled.

She hurried out of the room, but ten minutes later she was back again with the visitors in toe. Coincidentally, one of them happened to be an electrician, and Kit spoke to him so passionately about their plight that he offered to help them out for free.

'See,' said Albert under his breath, after he had shaken hands gratefully with the man. 'I said you had a way with people.'

* * *

Outside, Bard was working flat out in the
gardens. Privately, Kit didn't think there
was much he could do to tidy them up. The
Moonstone grounds reminded her of the
impenetrable, thorny scrub around the castle in
the story of the Sleeping Beauty. Surely it would
take months to hack it all back.

But she was wrong. Bard was a gardener of
great experience and he knew what to do. He
focused most of his energy on the front of the
house, trimming the trees, clearing away ivy and
weeding the gravel. Then he attacked the long
grass with a strimmer and mowed it smooth.

At the back of the house he took a different
approach and didn't even attempt to clear the
jungle. Instead, he made a feature of it, letting
the poppies riot amongst the long grass and
thistles. He cut some narrow paths through the
wilderness and positioned benches in especially
beautiful spots. Then he made some simple
wooden swings and strung them up from the
trees. When Kit tried one out, she felt as if she
was flying with the butterflies over a sea of
undulating green.

* * *

While Bard, Roz and Albert were busy with their projects, Kit dashed around the museum doing everything else. Unlike the other three, her work didn't end when the sun went down. She had the night shift to coordinate as well.

'Listen up you lot,' called Kit on the first night, when everyone had gathered in the hall. 'Tatyana and I have divided you into groups. Fenella, Claudia, Sir Jasper and Ping Xing will carry on in the sewing room, but the rest of you will be spread out over the museum. Fenella and Minna have copies of the list. You need to find your name and see which group you're in.' She touched the head of the little girl beside her, who now toddled forward with her sister and began proudly handing out sheets of paper.

'You've missed me off,' said Nurse Butcher, squinting through her glasses.

'I don't think so,' said Kit. She looked down at her own copy. 'You're in group E. You'll be cleaning the library with Winifred Ware, Harriet Harrow and Captain John.'

There was a disturbance on the stairs and the familiar, haughty voice of Lady Ann Hoops, sliced through the air. 'Over my dead body.'

She said. 'I will never allow anyone from the eighteenth century to be part of a mixed group.'

'And I certainly shall not countenance any of my people to work alongside hers,' retorted Kiko Kai from the other staircase, stabbing a finger in the direction of Lady Ann Hoops.

Down they swept, filling the room with their frosty disapproval. Winifred Ware hastily dropped her list on the floor and Minna sized Fenella's hand in fright.

Everyone started to shuffle and glance at each other uneasily and for a dreadful moment Kit thought she was about to lose them again. Then, out of the blue, Giles Clanker stomped forward. He yanked a duster out of Dorothy Dorsey's hand, clattered stiffly up the stairs and began jerkily polishing the grandfather clock.

'Bravo!' said Sir Jasper in an astonished voice. 'That fellow has the right attitude. Come along everyone, let's follow his example.' And everone immediately began putting on aprons and picking up buckets and brooms. Looking sour, Lady Ann Hoops and Kiko Kai retreated back up the stairs, and Kit whirled Minna round in relief.

It wasn't all plain sailing. The costumes required a lot of supervision and there were many dramas over the next few days. Harriot Harrow got stuck up a ladder. The African warrior accidently emptied a dustbin into one of the toilets and blocked it. Minna snipped a pile of dusters into tiny pieces and Sita Chakrabarti had to be banned from doing any polishing because she kept splitting her fragile silk sari.

Despite these issues, the restoration work progressed well, although Lady Ann Hoops and Kiko Kai continued to argue and make trouble whenever they could. Kit gave up hope that they would ever come to their senses. Some things, it seemed, were beyond repair.

Then at the end of the first week, Kit spotted a fatal flaw in her plans for Moonstone and forgot all about Lady Ann Hoops and Kiko Kai. For a whole twenty-four hours, she could think of nothing else, but at last she came up with a solution that she thought might work. The only problem would be getting her family to agree.

* * *

The first they knew about it was at breakfast on Friday the 21st, only seven days before the inspection. Kit spread butter on a slice of toast and said casually, 'So what are we going to do about the visitors?'

'What visitors?' said Bard stirring his tea.

'Well, that's the problem, isn't it,' said Kit.

'There aren't any. Won't it look weird if the museum is totally empty when the inspector comes to look round it?'

There was a long silence as the truth of this dawned on everyone.

'She's right,' said Albert at last. 'If we want to convince the council that Moonstone is a thriving success, then the place should be packed with tourists.'

'Well, I don't know what we can do about that,' said Bard.

There was another silence. Kit put her knife down carefully. 'I . . . I had a kind of idea,' she said.

'Oh, here we go,' chuckled Bard.

'I thought maybe we could have some kind of an event. You know, Bard, like the ones you had at Moonstone long ago, when our grandmother was alive. We could invite people to come, tell them it was to celebrate the reopening of the Costume Museum.'

Bard whistled. 'Oh I don't think it's going be possible to fix up something like that. We've only got a week left. There's not time enough to send out invitations, let alone make all the arrangements.'

'There's always social media,' suggested Albert.

'Al,' said Roz warningly. 'Don't get Kit's hopes up.'

'Well, why not? What's the point of doing all this work if no one is going to see it? I'm sure, between us, we can pull a guest list together. It doesn't really matter who we invite as long as they are human beings.'

'No one will be able to come at this short notice,' said Roz.

'Some will. We just have to make the guest list bigger and maybe throw in a free cup of tea or something.'

'Tea? Where are we going to get tea from?'

'I used to know a fella who ran a catering company,' said Bard. 'Could see if he'd be interested in putting up a tent in the grounds.'

'Good idea.'

Kit was pleased to see how well her family were responding to this new challenge. There was just one small point she needed to draw their attention to.

'And what about the reopening itself?' she said innocently.

'The reopening?'

'Yes, we'll need someone to come and make a speech . . . someone famous.'

Roz snorted. 'Kit, for God's sake. Isn't filling the museum with guests enough for you? You want a celebrity as well?'

'. . . and the press,' said Kit.

* * *

So now, on top of everything else, they had
a major event to organize and only seven
days to do it in. Soon Albert was managing a
last-minute advertising campaign and tracking
down a local celebrity who could open the
museum. Meanwhile Roz was up to her ears
with guest lists and caterers, and Bard was busy
preparing an area on the front lawn for a tea
tent as well as trying to sort out the car park,
which was knee deep in brambles.

With everyone so tied up with all this extra
stuff, it was becoming more difficult to keep
on track with the renovation work. Time was
running out and they were falling behind. There
was still a lot to do in the portrait gallery,
and it had taken Bard so long to find a way of
removing the burnt door blocking the summer
room that this last gallery had hardly even been
started.

Most of Kit's time, during the last few days,
was spent making a curtain that would cover
the fire damage in the portrait gallery. Fenella
was frantically trying to finish her own work

and had no time to help her, so Kit had to make the drape on her own. Her sewing skills had improved greatly, but it was a lot to expect of a beginner, and she only managed to complete the curtain the night before the opening.

'Well done, Kit,' said Bard when he had helped hang it in place. 'That looks a treat. You'd better pull it across the door and I'll go and find a No Entry sign to keep the public out of the summer room.'

'But I don't want to keep them out,' said Kit blankly

Bard was perplexed. 'It's a shame, I know, but I don't see how we can let anyone in there, looking the way it does.'

'There's not that much to do,' said Kit stubbornly. 'The walls could do with a sweep and the curtains need shaking and I've got to clean the floor and the furniture and all the windows, but there's nothing actually broken and the ceiling doesn't need painting.'

'Hardly anything,' said Bard reverting to sarcasm. 'Don't be daft. It's eight o'clock already and the museum opens tomorrow. You'll have to let this one go, Kit. I'm sure the inspector won't punish us because one gallery is closed.'

Kit didn't say anything but she felt mutinous. As far as she was concerned, the summer room was one of the best galleries in the museum, and there was no way she was going to let it go. She was sure that with the help of the others, they could prepare it in time. But when she examined it with Tatyana later on that night, she also shook her head. There was far too much to do, and by now the costumes had all put away their aprons and were preparing themselves for the big day tomorrow.

There was an atmosphere of excitement in the museum. It was like being backstage on the opening night of a new play. Every mirror in Moonstone had a costume in front of it, twirling around, checking to make sure that everything was perfect. Fenella and Claudia were rushing around with pins and needles, attending to last-minute tweaks, while the ballet dancer choreographed everyone's pose and Sir Jasper handed out the labels.

But somehow, Kit couldn't throw herself into it as she would have done normally. Eventually she left them to their primping and returned to the summer room alone. Perhaps if she worked flat out all night long, she could make the room passable. She fetched the ladder and a broom and made a start on the walls, sweeping the cobwebs and dust off as best she could. Soon her arms and neck were aching unbearably and she was so tired that her eyes were actually closing as she worked.

There was a sofa in one corner of the room. Maybe if she lay down for one of those ten-minute power naps Sir Henry was always going on about, it would give her the energy to carry on? Kit dropped onto it thankfully and, two seconds later, she was sound asleep.

CHAPTER 18

'She's here. Bard, Al, I've found her. Kit, for goodness sake wake up. We've been looking for you everywhere.'

Kit could hear her sister's voice but she had been so deeply asleep that she couldn't yet open her eyes. She was aware of movements and footsteps around her.

'What the ruddy heck has been going on in here?' That was Bard's voice.

'I know. She must have been working all night to get it looking like this. How did she get those costumes in here?'

'Ooo, she's a stubborn little old so-and-so. I told her to let this room be.'

'Do you know who she reminds me of? Dad!'

Kit prised one eye open a crack. She couldn't let that pass. 'I'm not,' she mumbled and forced her other eye to unglue.

She was lying on the sofa in the summer room, tucked up in a large dust sheet, while her brother, sister and grandfather stood around, looking concerned. Through the windows Kit could see the clear blue sky of a perfect summer morning.

She sat up suddenly, pushing off the dust sheet.

'Who washed the windows?' she demanded. Then she stared around at the rest of the room. It wasn't only the glass that was clean, the walls had been swept too and the floor and furniture had been polished. Even the fireplace looked immaculate.

'You did, idiot,' said Albert.

Kit opened her mouth and then shut it again.

'You must have worked all night,' said Roz. 'You even managed to move a couple of costumes in here.'

'I did?' Kit turned to look and there on a large plinth at the far end of the room was Lady Ann Hoops and Kiko Kai. They were standing side by side, their heads turned a little towards each other. What exactly had been going on here? Of all the mannequins in the museum, these were the last two she would have put on display together.

'I'd love to know how you got that old court mantua in here all on your own?'

Kit was still goggling at the two rivals. 'I... I don't know how. It's a . . . miracle.'

They walked back through the galleries in silence, gazing around at what they had achieved. Moonstone had changed out of all recognition. The floors and wood panelling that had once been so dull and dirty were now spotless and well-polished. The ceilings were clean and white. The broken furniture had been repaired and the windows were gleaming.

'How did you get this place so clean and tidy?' said Roz stopping suddenly and staring at Kit as if she'd only just noticed. 'And the costumes look amazing.'

Kit had to agree that they did.

'She's a little miracle-worker isn't she . . . just like her mum,' said Bard. He looked sideways at Kit and, just for a moment, she wondered if he was implying something more. 'I'm not sure about the positions you've put them in, though. We've always displayed things chronologically before, but you've got everything muddled up together. The mannequin over there in the yellow eighteenth-century frock looks like she's about to go off for a bike ride with that other one in the bloomers.'

'They've become very good friends,' murmured Kit.

'What?'

'I said I hope the inspector likes it.' At the thought of this mysterious figure, Kit's stomach fizzed with nerves, and it suddenly hit her that in six hours' time, the future of Moonstone would be decided once and for all.

* * *

Back in the flat the phone was ringing and Bard hurried into the office to answer it. He appeared a moment later looking troubled.

'That bloomin' celebrity you found to open the museum, Albert. She's only gone and pulled out. Says she can't come no more.'

'What?' shrieked Roz.

'Got food poisoning or something.'

'You're kidding,' said Albert.

Kit felt her legs go week and sat down—thump!—on one of the kitchen chairs. Then she did something completely out of character and burst into tears.

Bard was horrified.

'Oh, don't cry,' he said in a stricken voice.

'We'll sort something out, don't you worry.'

'But what can we do at such short notice?' asked Roz.

Kit looked pleadingly at Albert, but he shook his head.

'I'm not sure there is anything, I'm afraid. It was touch and go finding that celebrity in the first place.' He gave Kit a bracing hug. 'Look, it's not the end of the world. We can still go ahead with everything else. We'll just have to open the museum ourselves. I don't mind making a speech.'

'No,' said Bard firmly. 'We've got to do better than that, Albert. No offence, mind.'

'But who can we ask? There's only a few hours until the event starts.'

Bard didn't reply. He was looking out of the window. Then he smacked one fist into his palm as if he had just made up his mind about something.

'You leave it to me,' he said and he went into his office and closed the door, leaving his grandchildren looking mystified.

He stayed there for some time. When he finally came out again, he looked pale and a bit agitated. He touched Kit on the head briefly with one hand.

'That's sorted then,' he said. 'So there's no

need for you to worry no more.'

'Who on earth have you—'

But Bard shook his head and went off into the garden to do some last-minute mowing. It was clear that they were going to have to wait and see.

* * *

Just before two o'clock, Kit positioned herself in the nursery. Fenella and Minna stood proudly on display close by and she found their presence calming at such a nerve-racking moment. The nursery window had a good view out onto the front gardens and there was the tea tent on the lawn below. Then, with a prickle of excitement, she saw the first car arrive. It bumped slowly down the drive and pulled into the car park. One minute later, another vehicle appeared, and soon there was a steady stream of them.

The grounds began to fill up with visitors. Kit darted into the Long Walk see what was going on at the back of the house. There was a flutter of bright summer dresses amongst the tall grass. The sun was warm and the trees stood out dark against the blue sky. Bard's swings were all in use, flying backwards and forwards, and she could hear children laughing.

Kit checked her watch and hurried back to the nursery. The inspector was due any time now, but how would she recognize him? Would that man from the council, Graham Groid, come too? She tried to remember what he looked like and her eyes searched amongst the throngs of visitors.

'Kit,' said Roz, rushing into the gallery. 'Did you see the helicopter arrive?'

'Helicopter?'

'That's what Bard was doing all morning, mowing a helipad!'

'What?' Kit was distracted. She thought she'd just spotted a face down on the gravel that she knew.

'It must be Bard's mystery celebrity. Come on, let's go and see. Kit, are you listening?'

'I don't believe it,' said Kit furiously. 'What's he doing here?'

'Who?'

'Finn Scudder. Look.'

Roz came to the window.

'He's that ferrety looking man with the sunglasses. I don't know who that is with him though?' She pointed to a middle-aged lady carrying a clipboard.

'Hmmm,' said Roz uneasily. 'I have a feeling that might be the inspector.'

'Well that's not fair,' exploded Kit. 'What's the museum inspector doing with Finn Scudder? He'll try and influence her against Moonstone, I know he will.' Kit banged her hands down on the window sill. 'I've got to do something to stop him. We can't let this go wrong now.'

'Kit, where are you going?' demanded Roz. 'Look, I don't think you should interfere . . .'

But Kit wasn't listening. She was racing down the stairs, through the hall and out of the front door, almost colliding with the clipboard lady on the door step.

'Oh, sorry,' said Kit breathlessly. She decided there and then, that her best strategy would be to ignore Finn Scudder as much as possible, so she held out her hand to the woman and smiled brightly. 'Hello. Are you the museum inspector?'

'Er, yes. I'm Muriel Flood,' said the lady. She looked slightly taken aback at having her hand shaken by a twelve-year-old.

'I'm Kit. My grandfather looks after Moonstone.'

There was a snort behind her. 'Well, that's a matter of opinion,' said Finn Scudder. Kit pretended not to hear.

'If you could hold on a moment, I'll go and find him, so he can give you a tour. He's been looking forward to meeting you.'

'Don't bother,' said Finn. 'I'm here to show the inspector round. Graham Groid asked me to take care of her.'

'I don't need taking care of, thank you, Mr Scudder,' said the inspector. She was looking around in a perplexed kind of way. 'I must say, I'm a little surprised to see how busy Moonstone is. I was under the impression that the visitor numbers were on the low side.'

'They're non-existent,' butted in Finn. 'This place is usually about as buzzing as a derelict night club. Don't be fooled, these people aren't here by chance. They must have been bribed.'

Kit hesitated, then decided that honesty was the best policy. 'There's a sort of event going on,' she explained. 'We've restored the museum and today it's being reopened to the public.'

'Restored the museum! What, in three weeks? An old man and a little girl?' Finn bent double laughing, as if this was the funniest thing he'd ever heard.

'I think it sounds rather intriguing, myself,' said the inspector. 'I can't wait to see.'

'Oh, don't take any notice of this kid. She's having a laugh. Even if they had a team of professionals working twenty-four hours a day, there's no way this dump could be turned round in three weeks.'

He moved purposefully towards the door but Kit repositioned herself in front of it and looked at him for the first time. 'I'm not having a laugh, we have restored the museum,' she said. 'And I won't let you in until my Grandfather gets here. It's not your job to show anyone around Moonstone, Finn Scudder. You don't own it yet.'

'Yeah, but I will by the end of the week,' he sneered. 'Now stop mucking about and get out of our way. The inspector and I have got important business to attend to and I don't like having my time wasted by a stupid little brat who—'

'Is there a problem?' said a cool voice behind them.

Finn swung around on the newcomer. 'Why don't you mind your own business, mate?'

'But it is my business, as that is my daughter you are shouting at.'

Kit's eyes flew to the tall figure who had just arrived. 'Dad!' she gasped. 'What . . . what are you doing here?'

'I've come to reopen the costume museum of course,' said Sir Henry, as though this was the most obvious thing in the world.

'Bard asked you to come?' said Kit incredulously. 'And you agreed?'

'I felt compelled to come and see what you

have been doing for the last three weeks. I understand that you've been busy, Katherine.' She tried to read his expression. Was he angry with her? Did he really want to see what she'd been doing? What had Bard told him?'

Now he was holding out his hand to Muriel Flood.

'You must be the inspector,' he said. 'I'm delighted to meet you. I'm Bernard Trench's son in law, Sir Henry Halliwell. I was just about to ask my daughter, Katherine, to show me around the museum. She has been staying at Moonstone on vacation and helping her grandfather with the restoration work. Why don't you join us?'

'Oh, goodness,' said Muriel Flood, looking slightly flustered. 'Well, if you're sure, perhaps I will. Thank you.'

'Then I'm coming too,' said Finn aggressively and pushed past Kit into the hall.

Kit hesitated. Was her dad really asking her to show him and the inspector around? Did he know what was riding on this?

'Off you go, Katherine,' prompted Sir Henry gently. 'We are in your hands now.'

She took a steadying breath. 'OK,' she said. 'Let's start in the oriental Room.' She led the way across the hall and, doing her best not to look at Finn Scudder, she began giving her first ever tour of Moonstone.

Kit wasn't sure who she wanted to impress more—the inspector, or her dad. Her mouth was dry and she was shaking, but as the tour progressed, Kit began to relax. Soon, she was talking confidently about all the different objects in the galleries.

Throughout it all, she was aware of Finn Scudder lurking in the background. His expression changed every time she looked at him—shock, disbelief, fury. Kit took particular pleasure in taking them into the portrait gallery, where Captain John was looking very dapper alongside his portrait. There was no trace of the fire any more, and Kit had to hide a smile as Finn stamped around the room searching for evidence that he could not find.

'And these are my two favourite costumes,' said Kit, as the tour drew to an end and they entered the nursery. 'This one is called Fenella and that's her baby sister, Minna. They're the only children's clothes in the collection, so they're very special.'

'I love the fact that you have given them names,' said Muriel Flood.

Finn Scudder rolled his eyes. 'Give me strength,' he muttered.

'Oh, I didn't make them up,' said Kit. 'They're

real people. Fenella and Minna Silk-Hatton actually lived at Moonstone in the eighteenth century. And I like to think this is still their home.' Kit looked meaningfully into Fenella's eyes.

'You are astonishingly well informed for a child of your age,' said the inspector. They moved out of the nursery and onto the hall balcony. 'I can see that Moonstone is very important to you, and I can also understand why. It's a beautiful and fascinating little museum and it would be a crime to close it down.'

Kit stopped dead, put out her hand and clutched the inspector's arm. 'Do you mean—'

'Yes, I do,' nodded the inspector, smiling. 'I have made a decision, and the council will not be selling Moonstone. In fact I'll go further than that. I want to see what can be done about finding the place more financial support. It's a disgrace how underfunded this museum has been. I can't imagine how your grandfather has managed.'

Kit was too overcome to speak. She looked around for her dad. Sir Henry was standing by the window, smiling at her.

The only person who didn't look pleased about the news was Finn Scudder.

'I've had just about enough of this,' he snarled, elbowing Kit out of the way and squaring up to the inspector. 'Moonstone was as good as promised to me. The paperwork is done, the finance is in place. It's a done deal.'

'It is not a done deal and it was not promised to you, Mr Scudder,' said Muriel Flood crisply. 'The decision was always subject to an independent inspection, and that inspection I have now carried out.'

She moved off around the balcony.

'You can't do this,' bawled Finn, going after her.

'Oh, yes I can, and I wouldn't make a scene here if I were you, we appear to have an audience!'

Kit didn't understand what the inspector meant until she looked down, then she got a shock. The hall, which had previously been empty, was now jam-packed with visitors, who must have gathered there ready for the official opening. They had obviously heard Finn shouting, as every face down below was staring up at him. Kit knew just how that felt.

Finn stuck his chin out belligerently and opened his mouth to speak, but a man who looked suspiciously like a reporter, chose that moment to start taking pictures and he thought better of it.

'You haven't heard the last of this,' he hissed and, directing a poisonous look at Kit, he stormed off down the stairs.

'What a vile little man,' remarked the inspector as they watched him shoving his way roughly through the crowd and out of the front door. 'I can't think why Graham Groid had anything to do with him.'

'There's nothing he can do to change the council's mind is there?' asked Kit anxiously.

'Nothing at all,' said the inspector. 'Is that your grandfather waiting at the bottom of the stairs?'

Kit followed her pointing finger and saw Bard standing next to her brother and sister. All three of them were staring after Finn Scudder, looking confused.

'Quite a family party,' murmured Sir Henry, leading the way down the stairs. He stopped beside Bard. 'It's good to see you Bernard,' he said stiffly.

Bard looked awkward. 'Er, thanks for coming at such short notice.'

Sir Henry hesitated and then held out his hand to his father-in-law, and Bard finally took it. Kit hadn't realized she had been holding her breath and let out a sigh of relief. Perhaps this would be a new beginning for them all?

'Before I do the honours and open the museum,' said Sir Henry. 'I think Katherine has something she would like to share with you all.'

'Oh, what's that, then?' asked the old man.

Kit was beaming. 'It's good news,' she said. 'The inspector has looked round the museum and she thinks it's great. She says the council won't be selling it any more. We've done it, we've saved Moonstone!'

CHAPTER 19

The rest of the day passed like a dream. Sir Henry stood where he was on the stairs and made a speech, before officially reopening Moonstone Costume Museum. Afterwards the guests flocked through the galleries. It gave Kit such a thrill to see the place full of people for the first time and the costumes being admired as they ought. By the end of the day, the brand new comments book had more than sixty entries in it, and every single one of them was positive.

There was just one thing bothering Kit. Sir Henry still didn't know about the letter from William Siddis and she couldn't relax until she had come clean about it.

'Dad,' she said as they stood side by side

on the gravel drive, waving the inspector off. 'There's something I've got to tell you. Something really bad.' She took a big breath. 'I failed the entrance exam for Sidds again.'

'Yes, so I heard,' said Sir Henry drily.

'You know already?'

'Of course I know. Malcomb Clapper emailed me a copy of his letter while I was away.'

'Oh,' said Kit. There was a tense silence. 'Are you . . . are you very angry?'

'Yes, I am,' said Sir Henry and Kit's heart sank. 'But not with you, Katherine. I'm angry with myself. I see now that I made you feel like a failure and I'm truly sorry. William Siddis School does not deserve you.'

Sir Henry put his arm awkwardly round Kit and squeezed her shoulder. 'I'm so proud of you. And your mother would have been too.'

Kit was completely lost for words. Her mouth hung open stupidly. It was the first time her father had ever said he was proud of her.

Sir Henry cleared his throat. 'You'll be pleased to hear that I've managed to obtain you a place at St Leopold's. That was the school you wanted to go to, wasn't it? The one with a good art department?'

Kit nodded, still unable to speak.

'And I'd like... I'd like to apologize for

something else as well.'

'Something else?!' said Kit. Was this really her father talking?

'Yes. I don't think done a good job of providing you with a stable, happy home. I've been away too much and all that moving around can't have been easy for you or your siblings. Perhaps we need to make some changes.'

Kit's heart suddenly started to beat faster. There was something important she needed to ask her dad and this seemed the perfect moment to do it.

'Actually Dad, I've been thinking about that too and I've got a favour to ask.' She stopped and looked back at the old grey house with the ivy growing up the walls. 'It's about Moonstone. I can't turn my back on it now, and I can't leave Bard, either.'

Sir Henry looked suddenly worried. 'What exactly are you suggesting?' he asked slowly.

'I want you to let me come back here in the school holidays. All of them.'

Sir Henry seemed to heave a sigh of relief. 'I think that could be arranged, Katherine, if your grandfather agrees.'

'Really? That's brilliant. Thank you,' and she threw her arms around him. 'Oh yes, and there's one more thing, Dad. Maybe . . . maybe you could start calling me Kit?'

* * *

That evening, after the tea tent had been dismantled and the last visitor had left, Roz and Al made a delicious picnic and they carried it out into the grounds. It was dusk and a huge harvest moon hung low over the roof of the house, as if it was watching them.

Kit couldn't remember the last time her family had spent an evening together like this, and never one when they had been so relaxed. Sir Henry took off his jacket and tie and lay on the grass, while Al and Roz handed out the food. Kit sat beside Bard, lecturing him on how to look after the costumes while she was away.

'I can give them a dust when I'm back at half term, so your job is to leave them alone and make sure that the visitors don't touch them.'

'What do you think I'm going to—'

'And I want you to promise faithfully that you won't go putting any of them back in the store. And you mustn't ever mention burning them again. You've got to treat them as if they're actual people.'

'Are you sure you want this girl to come and stay with you in the holidays,' Roz asked Bard.

'She's turning into a fanatic.'

'Don't worry, I'm used to it. Your mum was just the same. She even made up names for the costumes. What was it she used to call that old mantua in the summer room? Lady Ann Frames or something. Oh, that reminds me,' he said suddenly. 'I've got something for you, Kit.' He felt in his pocket and brought out two tiny wooden dolls, with jointed limbs and exquisitely carved faces. 'I never got round to making the people for that doll's house of your mum's, so here's the first two. Thought you could amuse yourself while you're away by making their clothes. It's those two girls from the nursery that you're so fond of.'

Kit held the miniature versions of Fenella and Minna in her hand and thought they were the most beautiful things she had ever seen.

When they had finished eating, Sir Henry opened a bottle of champagne and filled everyone's glass. Then Bard stood up.

'I'd like to make a toast if that's all right.' He raised his glass so that it gleamed in the moonlight.

'To my family,' he said.

* * *

It was midnight and the inhabitants of the
costume museum were gathering in the great
hall when Kit arrived on the balcony. She could
see everyone down below and it reminded her
of the night she had met Fenella and witnessed
the magic of Moonstone for the first time. There
was a feeling of suppressed anxiety in the air
and she could hear agitated voices.

'Have you heard anything?

'Is there any news?'

'Oh, don't cry, Claudia. I'm sure it will be all
right.'

Kit ran towards the nearest staircase and
there was Fenella sitting on the top step waiting
for her. When she saw Kit, she rose to her feet,
trembling.

'It's OK,' Kit couldn't get the words out fast
enough. 'Moonstone is safe. Everything is going
to be fine.'

Fenella's pale face suddenly glowed with
happiness and relief. The two girls clasped
hands and danced round and round in dizzy
circles.

'We must tell everyone else,' said Kit when
they paused to catch their breath. Fenella
immediately dragged her round to the centre of
the balcony where she would be most visible.

'Oi!' shouted Kit as loudly as she could,

waving her arms in the air. 'Want to hear some good news? You've saved Moonstone.'

There was a moment of silence and everyone stared dumbly up at her as if they didn't understand English, and then suddenly they went wild. Minna jumped up and down on the spot. The African Warrior did a war dance. Giles Clanker strode jerkily round in circles at double the speed. Harriet Harrow grabbed the bicycle and began pedalling after him. The ballet dancer executed sixteen pirouettes without falling over, and Tatyana Kozlov actually smiled.

'And let that be a lesson to you all,' said a familiar, aristocratic sounding voice, 'That anything can be achieved, if you will only learn to work together.'

Kit scanned the agitated crowd below and her jaw dropped. This had to be the weirdest sight of all—Lady Ann Hoops and Kiko Kai walking together through the hall, arm in arm. They were bowing to right and left, as if they were single-handedly responsible for the saving of Moonstone.

'Ahh, here comes the child now,' said Lady Ann Hoops as she caught sight of Kit hurrying down the stairs to meet them. 'Impatient to thank us, no doubt.'

'And what a lot he has to thank us for,' said

the deep voice of Kiko Kai.

Lady Ann Hoops halted and looked at her companion.

'My dear Kiko, you surely know by now that it's a girl we are talking about not a boy.'

'Good heavens, is that so? I must say I always thought he was a boy with his funny hair and that peculiar stripy leg attire.'

Lady Ann Hoops shrugged slightly. 'Well, what difference does it make? The child still needs to thank us for spring-cleaning the summer room. What gruelling hard work it was.'

'And dangerous,' added Kiko Kai. 'That appalling moment when you nearly slipped off the ladder while polishing the windows. The shriek you gave. I shall never forget it to my dying day.'

'Oh, don't remind me,' shuddered Lady Ann Hoops. 'But not even that woke the child up. She just went on snoring away on the sofa. It was most off-putting. But some people are naturally lazy I believe.'

'I'm not lazy,' said Kit who had arrived at last with Fenella close behind her. 'I'd just been working so hard that I couldn't keep my eyes open.'

'Indeed,' said Lady Ann Hoops. 'Well

perhaps the people from your century are not accustomed to working as hard as we are. Why you didn't ask for our assistance sooner I cannot imagine.'

'Yes,' added Kiko Kai sweetly. 'We are always happy to help. You only have to ask.'

'But . . . but . . .' said Kit and then stopped. She could see that this was an argument she could never hope to win and, anyway, what did it matter? Lady Ann Hoops and Kiko Kai had made friends at last, that was the important thing. 'Thank you,' she said, 'The summer room looks amazing. You really did save the day.'

The two costumes smiled at her graciously.

'I have an announcement to make,' said Lady Ann Hoops imperiously. 'In honour of the occasion, I propose a little celebration. Let us have a costumes ball.'

'Oh yes, do let's,' said Kiko Kai. 'We haven't had one for an age.'

Everyone seemed equally enthusiastic and began dashing around, getting ready. Kit sat down on the steps, out of the way, wondering what a 'costumes ball' entailed. Soon the centre of the hall had been cleared and with some difficulty, a collection of musical instruments had been carried down from the salon above and arranged in a semicircle. Kit watched in fascination as the musicians took their places and after tuning up, began to play. Beatrice Bligh was plucking away on a harp, Sita Chakrabarti was playing the sitar, Winifred Ware was seated at the spinet, the Inuit man was a sensation on the fiddle, and Giles Clanker was on hand to provide procession.

In no time, everyone was dancing. It was all quite decorous at first, but as the evening progressed, the costumes started to really let their hair down. Soon Ping Xing and Claudia Clack were having a polka competition with Sir Jasper Stockings and Dorothy Dorsey. Kiko Kai was demonstrating how to perform a traditional Japanese dance to anyone who would watch. The gentlemen in dressing gowns were taking it in turns to waltz Lady Ann Hoops around the room. The ballet dancer was attempting to teach Tatyana Kozlov how to do an arabesque, while the vicar had hoicked up his robe and was doing some kind of cancan in the middle of the room.

Kit couldn't resist joining in and soon she, Fenella and Minna were careering around the hall having the time of their lives.

All night long the party carried on, but when the windows in the hall began to lighten Kit knew the time had come to say goodbye. The costumes gathered at the foot of the stairs to wish her well and thank her one last time.

Kiko Kai bowed her head and Lady Ann Hoops held out her hand graciously. This time Kit knew what was expected of her and she managed a perfectly creditable curtsy. Then she said a special goodbye to Claudia Clack, Ping Xing, Nurse Butcher Winifred Ware, Dorothy Dorsey and Captain John. Tatyana Kozlov surprised her greatly by throwing her arms around her and embracing her, and Sir Jasper was so overcome that he couldn't say goodbye at all. Then it was Minna and Fenella's turn. Kit picked up Minna and twirled her around in a circle before setting her down carefully on her feet and turning to Fenella.

'I promise I'll come back again soon,' she said. 'And I've had a brilliant idea about what we can do in the museum next time I'm here.' Kit lowered her voice so that no one else could hear. 'What do you think about opening a twentieth-century gallery at Moonstone? It would really give Lady Ann Hoops and Kiko Kai a run for their money!'

Fenella clasped Kit's hands and tried to smile, but her lips trembled and Kit felt her own eyes fill with tears. She had grown so close to Fenella, what would she do without her?

Through the windows the light was growing stronger. Soon the sun would rise and the magic of Moonstone would be lost. Kit squeezed Fenella's hands one last time and tore herself away, hurrying up the stairs. At the top, she paused to look back and could see Claudia Clack flourishing her handkerchief, before Sir Jasper seized it and buried his nose in it.

'Farewell,' they called. 'Come back soon.'

And then, just as Kit was turning away, she saw Fenella suddenly burst out of the crowd and race up the stairs towards her. Out of breath, she reached Kit at last and flung her arms around her.

'Goodbye, Kit,' she whispered in her sweet, husky voice. 'And thank you.'

Lara Flecker originally trained as a costume maker and after a brief spell working in the theatre and film industry, moved sideways into the museum world. She has spent 15 years as a senior textile conservation display specialist at the Victoria and Albert museum, is a leading expert in the display of fashion and dress, and is the author of *A Practical Guide to Costume Mounting*. *Midnight at Moonstone* is her first children's book, combining her love of storytelling and historic dress.

Trisha Krauss began her career as an illustrator in NYC. Her work has appeared in hundreds of publications including regular features for the New York Times. For the past 14 years she has lived and worked in London. Her first picture book, *Maude: The Not-So-Noticeable Shrimpton*, published by Puffin, was written by Lauren Child. Since then she has illustrated and written her own book, *Charlotte's Very Own Dress*, published by Random House and continued to work for a wide range of international clients.